To All Our Harlequin Friends,

Hummingbird Island is sent to you
with our sincerest best wishes for a
joyous holiday, and love and
happiness in the coming year.

Harlequin Reader Service
Christmas, 1982

Marcel had tried to poison her!

Fiona stood there, badly shaken. She knew then that Bill had been right when he said Marcel might prove to be a dangerous customer.

Now Bill had both hands on her shoulders, gripping her, steadying her. Fiona told him what had happened.

Bill swore softly and said, "How could I have been such a fool as not to expect something like this?"

Fiona's heart sang. It gave her a thrill to see how upset Bill was at hearing her news. Surely his reaction showed he cared for her a little.

Here I go again, Fiona thought ruefully, about to give my love to a man who doesn't want it. . . .

HUMMINGBIRD ISLAND

BY JILL TAHOURDIN

Harlequin Books

TORONTO • NEW YORK • LOS ANGELES • LONDON
AMSTERDAM • PARIS • SYDNEY • HAMBURG
STOCKHOLM • ATHENS • TOKYO • MILAN

This edition published December 1982

ISBN 0-373-83001-7

CHAPTER ONE

THIS MORNING, so early that breakfast was still hours away and none of the other passengers was astir, Fiona Leigh had been up on deck in time to see the liner shake off the blue waters of the Caribbean, and romp with the tide through one of the channels called the Dragons' Mouth into the gray green Gulf of Paria, heading for Trinidad.

Only two weeks ago, in early February, they had left England shivering under the snow, but here it was full springtime. The warm trade wind came singing over the water, and whipped through Fiona's short, curlyish dark brown hair as she leaned at the port rail, watching with delight the sliding panorama of little beaches, white villas, coconut plantations and orange groves.

"Well, there it is," said a pleasant male voice behind her. "Trinidad. Land of the hummingbird. What do you think of it, Fiona, my sweet?"

Fiona turned a sparkling glance to meet him. She knew he was amused by her naiveté, but she didn't mind.

"Oh, it's wonderful, Oliver," she exclaimed. "It looks just as exotic and exciting as I imagined. I know I'm going to love it."

"Hmm. Better wait and see what goes on behind the technicolor facade, don't you think? I suppose they'll be on the quay waiting for you?"

"You mean Dawn and Colin? Well, I certainly hope so," Fiona said with a little laugh.

"Lovely girl, Dawn," Oliver said offhandedly.

Oliver Hayne had met her stepsister, it seemed, on an earlier visit to the island. He was an architect, returning for consultation on a big oil-field project. A confirmed air traveler, he had come by sea this time to recuperate from an attack of influenza that had laid him low in England; and though Fiona, from the first moment, had mentally listed him under Professional Charmers, he had certainly helped her enjoy the voyage.

"Yes, Dawn certainly is lovely," she agreed warmly now.

Lovely and married to Colin. So what on earth has she found to be unhappy about, Fiona was asking herself.

Three years ago when Colin Murray was on leave from the big sugar estate he managed in Trinidad, she herself had fallen helplessly in love with him—a big, sandy-haired Scot, not a bit her type she would have said, with a lean, serious face, intensely blue eyes and an infectious dry humor.

He had seemed to enjoy being with her—sailing, or exploring the New Forest, or going up to London for dinner and a show, or just walking and talking. They had so much in common. But then Dawn came back home from a visit up north, and from the moment he met her Colin had eyes for no one else.

"When I marry, it's going to be for money," Dawn used to declare when she and Fiona were discussing young men and love, in the bedroom they had shared so amicably since the day—twenty years ago now—when Dr. Leigh had brought home Dawn's widowed mother as his wife. "Just *imagine* being a poor man's wife."

But in the face of Colin's dynamic courtship Dawn had forgotten all that. She hadn't even stopped to wonder if life on a West Indian sugar estate was going to

6

be the answer to her luxurious dreams. Radiant and couldn't-care-less, she had gone off with Colin to Trinidad (after searching in her old school atlas to find out just where it was).

"Everything's wonderful, Fiona," she had written ecstatically a few weeks later. "Such a glamorous island. And a great big house, with quite a romantic history, lots of servants, a marvelous husband, and such sunshine! If only you were nearer and could pop in for a chat like we used to have."

Poor Fiona, doubly bereft and thoroughly ashamed of the envy she couldn't quite manage to suppress, had had to take herself sternly in hand and cure herself of the painful raptures of unwanted love as best she could.

It wasn't easy. But time had helped, as time usually does. And she could even manage to laugh at herself now, remembering how her heart used to somersault at the sound of his voice.

Blessed Colin, to have offered her this journey, this chance of a job on the island of hummingbirds. She would be company for Dawn, he had written; Dawn was not happy.

She could hardly wait to see him and Dawn again.

BUT IT WASN'T COLIN, after all, who stood beside Dawn on the sunbaked quay, among a crowd of noisy cheerful people. The stepsister—fragile-looking, a little taller than Fiona, with long honey-colored hair, amber eyes and an exquisite golden tan—shrugged slender shoulders and gave a cool little laugh.

"Colin couldn't leave his precious sugar, not even to come up and welcome *you*, darling." Her voice was oddly deep, a little husky in tone and wholly enchanting. "So he sent his love and Bill Derwent, his field manager, to collect you. This is Bill. Bill, my stepsister, Fiona Leigh.''

Aware of a keen pang of disappointment that made her wonder if she'd been wise, after all, to risk seeing Colin again, Fiona shook hands with a dark-haired young man, not overly tall but somehow impressive, with an air of inner power and confidence. His eyes, steel gray in a lean brown face, looked down at her unsmilingly.

"How do you do, Miss Leigh. Pleasant voyage, I hope? I'll come along with you and see to your baggage, shall I?''

"Oh . . . you're very kind.'' She half turned from him as Oliver came up and joined them. "Look, here's somebody you've met before, Dawn.''

Oliver's eyes seemed drawn irresistibly to Dawn, whose face, with its new little air of discontent, was suddenly alight.

"Why, Oliver!'' she cried, and held out her hands.

"Hello, my dear. You look ravishing,'' Oliver said as he took both her hands and held them. "Oh—good morning, Derwent.''

"Morning, Hayne. Coming, Miss Leigh?''

Bill Derwent's voice, crisp with what she could only think was disapproval—of Dawn or Oliver or herself—was almost a command. Flushed, a little indignant, Fiona went with him to the customs area.

He certainly was efficient as he saw her through the routine formalities. Fiona found herself quite tongue-tied, as she walked back with him to rejoin Oliver and Dawn. As for him, he made no effort to entertain her with small talk.

"There, everything's aboard,'' he said in his firm, no-arguments-please voice. "Ready to start back now, Dawn?''

But Dawn had other ideas.

"Bill dear, how often do I escape to Port of Spain?" she protested. "And now that I'm here, what's the big hurry? Oliver's fixing everything. He's invited us all to the hotel for lunch, and then he'll drive us up Lady Chancellor Hill. Fiona really ought to see the view from there. Once she gets to Cassia and in Colin's clutches, she'll see and hear nothing but sugar, sugar, sugar for the rest of her stay. You'll join us, won't you, Bill?"

She laid her hand on his forearm for a moment, and Fiona noticed how he almost jerked it away. The beguiling look Dawn gave him from under her long, gold-tipped lashes seemed to have no effect on him at all. *I believe he actually dislikes her,* thought Fiona, scandalized.

"Thank you, no," he replied evenly. "You know I can't spare the time. And Colin's expecting us all for lunch at the Great House. Mrs. Murray's coming over, too, had you forgotten? We'd better get going if we're not to be late."

There was a determined spark now in Dawn's eyes.

"Nonsense, Bill," she retorted. "Fiona wants to stay, don't you, darling?"

Fiona hesitated, embarrassed. She thought the luncheon party would be fun, and she did rather want to see the famous view. She also considered that Bill Derwent was being unduly brusque and bossy. But she didn't want to offend Colin or his mother—who according to Dawn was a lady of formidable character.

In the face of Bill Derwent's penetrating derisive scrutiny she stammered, "Well, I . . . don't you think, perhaps . . . ."

But Oliver cut in smoothly. "I'm sure Derwent will explain to Colin and Mrs. Murray."

"No, really, Oliver, I . . ." Fiona began; but Dawn took her arm and whispered, "Come on, pet, don't argue."

Whereupon Bill Derwent said curtly, "Just as you like, of course, Dawn. I take it Hayne will drive you down then." And with a "So long" that wasn't directed at anyone in particular, he slid into the front seat of the station wagon and drove off.

"Phew," Oliver murmured. "There goes a character who certainly doesn't approve of you, my sweet."

But whether he meant herself or Dawn, Fiona couldn't be sure.

Now they were leaving the dusty quay and the old harbor crowded with tall-masted schooners and sloops, and were driving in the sizzling noonday heat through a big square, and into narrow streets packed with shoppers and vehicles, and ringing with canned music and mellow West Indian voices.

Amused at Fiona's wide-eyed absorption in the passing scene, Oliver told her, "Just wait till Carnival time next month. Port of Spain is really something then."

The hotel, white and aggressively modern, faced onto the savanna—an open grassy space. Fiona gazed around her with lively interest, thinking what a cosmopolitan crowd it was, and listening with delight to the French, Spanish, Portuguese, British, American and even Chinese voices that filled the air.

Dawn, armed with a tall glass of planter's punch clinking with ice, was obviously enjoying herself now. She had become gay and animated, just like her old self, Fiona thought with pleasure.

But she and Oliver lingered so long over their drinks, and then over luncheon—that Fiona, eager to get her first look at Cassia in full daylight, began to be afraid they wouldn't reach it before evening.

She sat quietly, looking around her while they chatted happily on and on, over their coffee, mostly about things and people unknown to her. Perhaps Dawn realized that she was being neglectful, for she suddenly stubbed out her cigarette and said gaily, "Well, how about Lady Chancellor? Ready to move on, Fiona?"

"Yes, please." Fiona got up quickly, before Dawn could light up again. She was smoking a lot, in quick nervous puffs; she'd never done that in the old days.

They drove around the savanna and up a long winding hill between high grassy banks. At the top of the hill they left the car and walked to the vantage point, a sort of platform that had been leveled off.

"Goodness, that really is a view," cried Fiona.

Far below she could see Government House enclosed in the lovely glade of the Botanical Gardens. In front of it stretched the savanna, and beyond that the town, dimly pastel colored under a shimmer of heat.

"When you've been in Trinidad a bit longer," Dawn said rather acidly, "you'll find you can't live on a view. Cassia's got a view, and heavens, how sick I am of it. Oh, well, let's go, Oliver, shall we? I know Fiona's pining to see the place. And Colin is probably fussing by now."

Fussing? It didn't sound in the least like the calm, seldom-ruffled Colin she had known, Fiona thought.

They swept down the hill, presently left the tangle of fine buildings and unbelievable slums that is Port of Spain, and drove eastward under a fathomless, cloudless sky. Fiona sat in front with the sunny-faced driver, Dawn and Oliver behind.

For a couple of miles the road ran between lines of crazy wooden shacks. Farther on were villages shaded with palms and breadfruit trees, where vendors displayed stalls of glowing tropical fruits whose names Fiona didn't know.

Beyond the small town of Arima they turned sharply northward to face the high forested ranges. Now the road ran across a broad sloping plain, planted thickly with sugar—an immense vista of tall green fronds, waving above robust jointed canes, and rustling harshly in the breeze like sheets of sandpaper being rubbed together.

"It's the cutting season," Dawn said. "Turmoil, my dear. Nobody thinks or talks of anything but the crop."

"Do they still cut by hand?" Fiona asked in surprise.

"Yes. Machine cutting damages the roots, and it's from the roots that the ratoons, the new canes, spring up, so they have to be handled tenderly," Oliver explained.

"It looks rather primitive," Fiona said, thinking of the combine harvesters she had seen in Hampshire, and the efficiency with which they cut and bundled and stacked.

"Trinidad *is* primitive," Dawn said, so bitterly that Fiona looked at her in surprise. But she went on in her ordinary voice. "Look, there's the Great House, right ahead through the big gates. Pretty tatty, isn't it?"

"Oh, Dawn, no. Picturesque, but not tatty," Fiona protested. She thought the huge, mellow old plantation house was lovely. A broad flight of steps led up to the balcony that ran around three sides of the house, and the flattened roof was of gray shingles. Purple bougainvillea, honeysuckle, jasmine and passion vine draped it in beauty and screened the interior from the sun's heat.

"Oh, and look, can these be hummingbirds?" Fiona went on excitedly, pointing to a bush covered with the creamy trumpets of moonflowers, above which tiny, brilliant, jewel-feathered creatures darted and quivered.

"Yes, they are," Dawn told her indifferently. "And that delicious aroma you notice is boiling sugar. It'll go on for weeks now. It'll pervade the air until you'll taste it in everything you eat and drink. Ugh, how I hate it!"

Colin came out onto the veranda as the car drew up. He was still in his working rig of open-necked shirt and shorts, which made him look longer and leaner than ever.

He shook hands with Oliver and offered him a drink. He kissed Dawn affectionately and hoped she'd enjoyed the drive. Then he turned to Fiona.

"Welcome to Cassia, Fiona. It's grand to see you again," he exclaimed, and gave her a warm brotherly hug of genuine welcome.

"My mother was sorry to miss you," he added, "but she had a bridge party this afternoon, so she couldn't stay on. She'd like you both to go over and have coffee with her tomorrow morning."

"That'll be lovely," Fiona said. Though she had felt a warm thrill of pleasure at seeing Colin again, she had been immensely relieved to find that her heart didn't pound and her knees shake at his touch as they used to do.

Thank goodness, I'm over him, she told herself.

Studying Colin, she found him older looking and thinner, with lines of strain around his eyes and mouth; and wondered whether it was worry about Cassia or about Dawn, that had put them there.

But he was still the same Colin, the nicest man she

13

had ever known. His face creased into its old amused expression as he lisened to her hilarious account of the voyage.

"You'll have to excuse me now," he said after a half hour of talk. Dawn made a resigned face, and Fiona hoped he hadn't noticed it. "I just ran over from the factory, to see if you'd arrived. We're in the midst of crop—not much time for anything else, actually, while it's on. But when Dawn has shown you your room, and you've had some tea, Bill Derwent will come over with a jeep and run you around the place, and show you the dispensary."

"Lovely, I'm longing to see everything," Fiona said in her enthusiastic way. She couldn't help noticing the bored, exasperated little shrug Dawn gave as her eyes sought Oliver's. *What's the matter with her,* she wondered again. *She never used to be like this, so bored and bitter and sort of uninterested. And she was so terribly in love with Colin when she married him, yet you'd think she didn't care a row of pins for him now. Can Oliver have anything to do with it? She certainly seems attracted . . . .*

"You'll stay on for dinner, of course, won't you, Oliver?" Dawn was saying, Colin having hurried off to the factory again.

She got her way, of course, and then she took Fiona up to see her room. It was big and airy, with slatted jalousies at the tall windows and a balcony from which you could look across the green waves of canes. A big negro woman had already started to unpack Fiona's suitcases and was pressing her dresses. *Oh, bliss,* Fiona thought—before hanging them in the closet.

"This is Heloise. She'll do your laundry and mend-

14

ing,'' Dawn said. Heloise paused in her unpacking and ironing to give the visitor a welcoming smile.

"How do you do, Miss Fiona,'' she cried. "I see your face is well shined.''

Seated in front of the chintz-draped dressing table that matched the bed, Dawn studied her perfect face in the glass and ran a comb through her silken hair. "I do hope you'll be comfy here, darling, and not too bored with the place,'' she murmured.

"Bored? Here—with you and Colin? How could I be? Why, I'm absolutely thrilled.'' Impulsively she rushed on. "What's wrong, darling? Are *you* bored?''

"Horribly, my dear, most of the time. There's nothing to do here, except listen to people talking endless shop about sugar. And there's nobody to have fun with. Colin just isn't among those present most of the time. You must have noticed he's wedded to his work. Thank heaven Oliver has come back. We must see a lot of him. He's an absolute angel, isn't he? I bet you fell for him on the voyage.''

Fiona laughed, refusing to commit herself about Oliver. "This Bill Derwent, what about him?'' she asked curiously. "He's rather an alarming person, isn't he? Don't you like him, Dawn? Or doesn't he like you?''

Dawn was smiling. "Perhaps he does like me, darling—rather too much,'' she said casually.

So that's it, Fiona thought flatly, *Bill Derwent is in love with her. Well, it could be. If he knows she cares nothing for him, that could account for the antagonism in his manner. And it's just what I might have expected. Colin, Oliver, now Bill Derwent. Dawn always did have that effect on men, ever since school days. . . .*

Fiona admonished herself in sudden impatience. The

thing to do was to fix her mind on her new job as dispenser at the clinic on the estate and on finding out as quickly as she could what was wrong with Dawn. That, she reminded herself severely, was what she was here for. . . .

They wandered downstairs presently to join Oliver, who was just finishing a telephone call to his hostess at the oil field, explaining that he was unavoidably delayed and wouldn't be in time for dinner. He could get away with murder, Fiona thought, amused, as the pleasant voice lied so charmingly.

There was a hail from outside, and Bill joined them.

"Come and have some tea, Bill, dear," Dawn said sweetly, smiling as she busied herself at the table.

How pretty she still is, Fiona thought lovingly, watching Dawn's graceful movements with silver teapot, milk jug and sugar tongs.

"Thanks, I will. Milk and two lumps, please," Bill said briskly. "The jeep is outside, Miss Leigh."

"Oh, for heaven's sake! Miss Leigh! How terribly pompous that sounds, Bill. Nobody ever calls Fiona, Miss Leigh," Dawn said, bursting out laughing. Fiona laughed, too, and the edge of a smile flickered, rather attractively she thought, over the poker face of Bill Derwent.

"I see. Well," he said, drinking his tea and setting down the cup, "I'm ready when you are—Fiona."

"Thanks, Bill, I'm ready now." Fiona smiled up at him, pleased by the discovery that he could be human, after all.

A SUGAR ESTATE, she discovered further, as they rattled along rough earth roads with the dry papery rustle of the sugarcane for accompaniment, is a little world in itself.

Leaving the Great House they had driven by the pleasant bungalows of the field, office, medical and laboratory staff; past the big sprawling factory and refinery; then by the cottages of the clerks and overseers, and the wooden barracks of the laborers.

"Good evening, sir," some called out in loud, genial voices, and the field manager honked his horn in reply.

Fiona was surprised to see that he was grinning cheerfully, and that the grin had carved a deep dimple in the cheek nearest to her. That made him seem more human, too.

"You must always honk," he explained. "If you don't the laborers take offense. 'Blow your horn,' they shout indignantly. The workers look on it as a polite greeting."

Fiona gave him a friendly smiling glance, thinking how much nicer he was than she had at first thought him.

"I'm looking forward to getting to know everyone better—when I start work in the dispensary, I mean."

"I only wish your sister . . ." he began, then abruptly changed the subject. "Those aren't so good," he said, pointing to a long line of tumbledown huts.

"Why, they're made of orange crates nailed together," Fiona cried.

"Yes, and a few dried palm leaves for thatch," Bill said soberly. "You can imagine what they're like in the rains. The trouble is, these workers are only seasonal—they just drift in at crop time, and then go off again. Colin plans to build permanent quarters for them, but the estate can't stand the expense yet. He's

17

only pulled it out of the red in the last two years. He's done wonders, you know. Bit of a change since the old slave days when his ancestors owned the place.''

"Why—I didn't know that."

"You didn't? Of course, he's only the manager now. But a Murray ancestor received a 'grant of broad acres' around 1810. Know your history, Fiona? That was just after our Admiral Harvey fought a Spanish squadron in the gulf, and Trinidad fell to the British.''

"And then?"

"Oh, well, sugar was king, as they used to say, for a long spell. Then it declined, slavery was abolished, and the rich planters gradually went down and down, till they were forced to sell out as and when they could. Colin's family hung on and were finally bought out by a big syndicate before the first world war. But Colin still feels about Cassia as if it was the family estate.''

They turned onto a narrow road between the blocks of cane. The jeep bumped and rattled over ruts and stones. It wasn't comfortable but Fiona was too interested to mind.

"Colin has devoted heart and soul to Cassia," Bill Derwent said suddenly, with great emphasis. "It'll kill him, honestly, if he has to leave it."

"But—is there any possibility he'll be leaving?"

"Don't you know?" he demanded roughly. "Have I got it all wrong? I thought you were in on this with Dawn. In fact I thought your arrival was all part of the plot. Are you telling me you don't know how she hates it here? How she never gives Colin any peace, nagging at him to throw up his job here and go back home to England? *Home. This* is home to Colin. He was born out here, you know. This is where he belongs. Dawn has no right to —''

18

Fiona broke in on him.

"Look, Bill, I didn't know all this. Until Colin wrote and asked me to come out here—because Dawn was a bit homesick and nervy, he said—I had no idea she wasn't perfectly happy. She certainly gave no hint in her letters to the family. And I don't feel I know you well enough yet," she went on with spirit, "to discuss my sister with you. She—there may be reasons you don't know about. I'd prefer to hear her side first. . . ."

"Do," he said shortly. Then he added more gently, "I'm sorry if I've misjudged you, Fiona, but I've been feeling pretty angry about all this, you see. Colin's the finest man I've ever known, and things are difficult just now. . . ."

"Difficult? In what way?"

"Oh—trouble's brewing on the estate, we all know that. Somebody is working among the labor, and we haven't found out who, yet. A paid agitator, probably, or more than one perhaps. It's so easy for that sort of chap to filter in among the crowd of seasonal workers, unnoticed."

"But can't you do anything?" Fiona asked, troubled and more than a little alarmed by all this.

"Of course we can," Bill said in that decisive voice of his, so full of inner confidence and strength. "Trouble can always be met and handled. But it never makes it easier to have women around playing you up, especially women like . . . what I mean is, Fiona, Colin oughtn't to have this other trouble to cope with, as well. If women aren't prepared to help, they shouldn't come out here." She saw that a flush had risen under the brown of his lean face. He was biting his lower lip, as if keeping back even harsher words.

"Please let's go and see the dispensary," Fiona said

abruptly. She was angry now, as well as upset. Bill Derwent had no right to voice criticism by implication.

"As you wish," he said, then swung the jeep around another sharp corner and drove on in silence. His manner as he showed her around the clinic was strictly impersonal. All sign of friendliness was gone from his voice.

She didn't, Fiona reflected, feel very friendly toward him, either. Her delight in the up-to-date dispensary and the neighboring laboratory, dental office and hospital went unexpressed.

She had come near to liking Bill Derwent very sincerely that evening; now a feeling of antagonism chilled her as she thanked him outside the steps of the Great House where he dropped her again. Life at Cassia, Fiona decided as she ran up the steps, was going to be a much more complicated affair than she had imagined.

The thought didn't diminish the zest with which she looked forward to it, nor the exhilaration, rather than dismay, with which she planned to do battle with Bill Derwent, both on her own account and on Dawn's.

CHAPTER TWO

THERE WAS NOBODY around. Dawn and Oliver weren't on the veranda—gallery they called it here, Fiona remembered—or in the garden.

So she wandered over the shining parquet of the salon, through a high archway into the large room beyond that faced west and was not flooded with the rosy amber light of sunset. From the window she saw one of the servants, a man called Cupid, talking to a stranger, a tall, slim man with a *café-au-lait* complexion. He wore tinted glasses and European clothes that sat on him rakishly.

His expression was arrogant and somehow menacing. No wonder Cupid, poor little man, looked so scared. He stood there wringing his hands and shaking his head—obstinately refusing, it seemed, to do whatever it was the tall man demanded of him. When at last the latter went off, seeming to breath threatenings and slaughter, Cupid stood for a while looking after him. He had an air of collapse, like jelly left in a too warm room. . . .

It was all very odd, and Fiona wondered if she should mention it to Colin or Dawn. Perhaps not, she decided. It was no affair of hers.

When Dawn came in, she brought Oliver Hayne with her. They had a predinner drink after Colin arrived at the end of his day's work, then the women and Colin went upstairs to change.

Fiona, coming down first in her pretty pale green organza, couldn't help smiling with pleasure when

Oliver exclaimed, "You look cool as a snowdrop, my sweet."

Dinner passed agreeably. Oliver was the sort of guest who would always be a hostess's delight. He talked easily and amusingly, and Dawn, under his spell, seemed for a time to have recaptured some of her old spontaneous gaiety. As for Fiona, everything was novel and delightful to her. She ate each course with frank enjoyment; but Dawn merely toyed with the food on her plate, then lighted a cigarette and puffed on it till the rest of them had finished.

Though Colin looked at her in a worried way more than once, he made no comment, but when his eyes chanced to meet Fiona's, he gave a rueful shake of his head as if to ask, "What do *you* make of it?"

Afterward they drank coffee in a corner of the gallery. The air was scented with jasmine and frangipani and honeysuckle; a fresh little breeze had sprung up and blown the sickly sugar stench right away.

It was all so delightful, so glamorous. *Lucky Dawn,* Fiona thought again. *All this—and Colin, too. She seemed to have everything to make her happy. And yet she evidently wasn't. Why? If only Dawn would tell her. Perhaps she would; at home, they had usually told each other most things sooner, or later. . . .*

Oliver had finished his coffee and cigarette. Now he rose reluctantly from his chair.

"I'm afraid I must take to the road," he said. "It's probably high time I reported to my kind hostess down south. No, don't move, please, any of you. My car's waiting."

Colin grunted in relief when he had gone.

"Well, now that we've got rid of Hayne, we can really talk," he said comfortably, settling down in his chair and starting to fill his pipe. "What on earth possessed you, Dawn, to ask him for dinner on Fiona's first night here?"

Fiona was amazed—and indignant—when Dawn replied in her husky enchanting voice. "Darling, didn't you realize that Oliver and Fiona have been terrific buddies on board ship? I simply hadn't the heart to send Oliver away."

"Oh . . . I see," Colin said. His voice held a note of doubt and—yes—*disappointment*. She felt her color rise and was furious with herself. Now he would certainly think—as Dawn, for reasons of her own, apparently meant him to—that she was in love with Oliver or Oliver with her or both.

Which was stupid and embarrassing and untrue and . . . . "Oh, bother," Fiona muttered to herself, feeling upset, "if only I can get a few minutes alone with Dawn, I'll have it out with her."

Colin began to talk about Fiona's job at the clinic, and the people with whom she would be working. The doctor was a grand person, a Scot like himself—she'd be meeting him tomorrow.

The rest of the evening passed pleasantly, and before she knew it, Fiona was quite ready for her bed. The long day, so full of new and exciting experiences, had been more tiring than Fiona had realized.

She and Dawn went up together, arms affectionately linked. She half expected Dawn would come into her room with her, flop on the bed and chat cozily in the old heart-to-heart fashion.

But all Dawn did was remind her about tucking in the mosquito net all around, give her a small hug and say with more real warmth than she had so far shown, "It's lovely having you here, darling. Sleep well, and don't get up till you feel like it. Heloise will bring you some tea and fruit when Colin's gone. Good night. God bless.''

She was smiling as she went out, but it was a strained smile, with none of the old gaiety. Fiona noticed how much thinner she was and lay awake for a long time, puzzled and bothered.

THE NEXT MORNING she rose and took a shower, after she had finished the tea Heloise provided. Then donning a crisp cotton dress and white sandals, she went downstairs to the breakfast table on the gallery.

Dawn came down a few minutes later and they breakfasted together, with Cupid in assiduous attendance. Dawn seemed in fairly good spirits.

"I'm going to cut some flowers for the house now," she said. "Would you like to help me arrange them afterward?"

"I'd love to. I say, Dawn," Fiona went on, abruptly changing the subject, "why on earth did you try, last night, to give Colin the idea that Oliver and I were . . . were . . . .''

"In love? Oh, that," Dawn replied airily, with her cool little laugh. "Why not? You don't want Colin to think you're still carrying a torch for him, do you, pet?''

Fiona stared at her in horror.

"You don't mean—Colin—you—*knew*?" she gasped.

"Why, of course, everybody knew," Dawn told her calmly as she cut a long-stemmed flower. "It stuck out a mile. Not that Colin ever said a word," she added hastily, seeing the distress on Fiona's telltale face. "But I say—don't tell me you still are?"

"Of course not, idiot. Would I have come out here if

24

I were? I got over him ages ago, " Fiona protested vigorously. To keep her own end up she went on. "If Oliver's in love with anyone, I'd say it's with you."

"That's what Colin—and Bill Derwent—seem to think," Dawn agreed complacently. "And that's why I want them to think it's you. Because I intend," stated young Mrs. Murray firmly, "to see just as much of Oliver as ever I can. If Colin sees fit to deprive me of his company for about seventy-five percent of the time, he can't blame me if I turn to somebody else. Oliver's a sweetie. . . ."

Fiona broke in anxiously, "You don't mean—*seriously,* Dawn? Oliver's a dear, but a bit of a butterfly, I think. Whereas Colin . . . ."

"One in a million," Dawn said with bitterness.

"Dawn, do tell. What's gone wrong between you and Colin? Why are you so . . . ."

But Dawn said coaxingly, "Now don't fuss, darling. And to please me, be a sport and try to look coy, instead of indignant, when I pretend to Colin that it's you Oliver comes to see."

Fiona opened her mouth to protest, but Dawn had gathered the cut flowers into her basket and was walking away.

So Dawn didn't mean to confide in her, it seemed. How changed she was, so hard and flippant and—unloving. What could have happened to make her like this?

"You'd better brief me," she told Dawn a few minutes later as they filled vases and bowls. "I'm rather scared, you know, at the idea of meeting Mrs. Murray."

"And well you should be," Dawn told her frankly. "She's a holy terror. Mamma-in-law is quite the most outspoken woman I've ever met. She's afraid of nothing and nobody. The heroine of the oil riots of way back.''

"What on earth do you mean?"

"Oh, never mind, you'll hear soon enough. Of course, one has to admit she's a marvel. Colin thinks the world of her. But she disapproves of me.''

"Disapproves?" cried Fiona indignantly.

"Indeed, yes. You see she'd planned from his childhood for Colin to marry the daughter of a neighboring sugar estate. Another sugar baby, you might say,'' said Dawn with a little grin. "Mrs. Murray was terribly grieved when her son returned from England with me in tow.''

"She ought to have been delighted,'' Fiona said loyally.

"Thanks, darling. But she wasn't. And now there's the other thing. . . .''

"The other?"

"No babies,'' Dawn answered succinctly, then went on to talk so firmly and decisively about flower arrangement that Fiona had no choice but to follow her lead.

They set off later, wearing shady hats to protect them from the sun, along the avenue to the little house where Colin had installed his mother after his marriage.

After his father's death, she had lived with him at the Great House, Dawn told Fiona; but she was not the sort of old lady who could tolerate a house with two mistresses and had insisted on leaving as soon as her daughter-in-law had settled in.

She was in the garden when they arrived—a small, spare, upright woman, with eyes blue like Colin's, but sharp as needles.

"Well, my dear, so this is your stepsister,'' she began briskly, giving Dawn a peck on the cheek, and shaking hands with Fiona. "You're not much alike—but of

26

course I remember there's no blood relationship between you, is there? Well, I hope you're going to like it here, Fiona, and persuade Dawn to make an effort to do the same."

Dawn seemed not to notice the severity of Mrs. Murray's look and manner. She asked urgently, "Mother, what was that song the gardener was singing? You can hear it all day. Something about fire in the mountain, but I can't catch all the words."

"That's what it's called: 'Fire in the mountain.' It's an old song and a bad one. When the laborers sang it in the old days, it used to mean they were planning mischief."

"Mischief? What sort of mischief?" Dawn's face, Fiona saw, had gone quite pale.

Mrs. Murray placidly poured out coffee, added cream and sugar, and got up to place a cup beside Fiona and another beside Dawn. "It's what they used to sing when they were planning to fire the cane fields."

"B-but, mother, do they mean that now? Does Colin know about this?" Dawn asked in a voice that shook.

Mrs. Murray glanced at her daughter-in-law. "Now don't get all worked up," she admonished. "Naturally Colin knows. And so does Bill Derwent. They've doubled the fireguard and taken all precautions. But you can't watch a place the size of Cassia at every danger point. Ah, well, we can only wait and see. It's happened before and no doubt it'll happen again. No good ever came of being scared before the event. Now, my dear, I know you'll like to see my new climbing rose. It's just coming into flower. Go and see it while I talk to your sister."

It seemed to Fiona that Dawn was glad enough to escape. She would have liked to go herself, but those bright blue eyes were fixed on her face.

"I wanted a chance to have a word with you alone," Mrs. Murray was saying calmly. "I'm going to be very candid with you, Fiona. Your sister is proving a poor sort of wife for my son. She refuses to give him children—"

"Oh, but Mrs. Murray," interrupted Fiona, in arms at once, "are you sure? Dawn always used to say that when she married she meant to have half a dozen children. People don't always have babies just when they want to . . . ."

Her voice trailed into embarrassed silence, for Mrs. Murray had put on a pair of gold-rimmed spectacles, and was surveying her grimly over the top of them. It made Fiona feel like a schoolgirl on the mat before the principal.

"I am aware of the facts of life," the old lady told her crisply. "And another thing. She continually urges my son to give up the management of Cassia in order to take her to live in England. Now you look a sensible sort of girl. Not a spoiled beauty like Dawn, thank heaven, though you're quite as pretty as is good for you. I want you to make her realize where her duty lies. Give her a good talking-to. . . ."

But that was too much for Fiona.

"Please, Mrs. Murray, Dawn is my sister," she broke in bravely. "I'm hoping she's going to feel happier, less homesick, now that I'm with her. But you mustn't ask me to interfere in what isn't, after all, my business."

Her eyes were bright with indignation. *Now I've done it,* she thought. *But I don't care. How dare she?*

To her surprise she saw that the old lady was smiling.

"Good girl," she said. "It's a pity Colin didn't choose you instead of Dawn, if he had to bring a-an outsider to the island. But there, men are like that. Well, just do the best you can with her. Some more coffee? No? Well, then, we'll go out and see the roses. This way. . . .''

Fiona followed her out to where Dawn stood moodily smelling a deep red *Etoile de Holland*. She was wondering how big a part Mrs. Murray had played, with her talk of fires and plotted mischief, in turning Dawn against the island she had thought so romantic and glamorous at first sight. The old lady had seemed to positively relish Dawn's nervousness and had said little to reassure her. She certainly was a bit of a tartar, thought Fiona.

She said nothing of this to Dawn, however. As they started to walk home, a jeep drew up with Bill Derwent at the wheel.

"Good morning," he said. "Can I offer you a lift? It's hot for walking."

"Oh, thank goodness, Bill dear. I'm exhausted," Dawn said dramatically.

Fiona was quite taken aback to see Bill Derwent's left eyelid droop toward her in an unmistakable wink. It confirmed her suspicion that he was human, after all.

"Been visiting Mrs. Murray? How was she?" he asked.

"In her usual cracking form," Dawn told him derisively.

He shook his head at her.

"Now, now, Dawn, admit she's a wonderful old lady."

"Oh, marvelous. And now, no doubt," Dawn went on resignedly, "you'll want to relate to Fiona the story of mamma-in-law and the rioters."

"Why, hasn't she heard it?"

"No, please tell me," said Fiona, smiling.

"When she was staying down on the oil fields with her daughter Marjorie, years ago now, she quelled a whole mob of rioters single-handed," he said. "When they came around the bungalow, drunk and clamoring for the servants to join them, she went out alone on the gallery and read them such a homily that they slunk off like the proverbial whipped curs. I can just imagine her," he finished with a grin.

"Me, too," said Dawn with feeling, and Bill laughed out loud.

Fiona, sitting behind Bill, studying the back of his head, liking it and the way his thick dark hair grew above the strong brown column of his neck, found it difficult to go on being annoyed with him.

Evidently he wanted to be friends, too, for when Dawn had run up the steps onto the gallery, and he was helping Fiona out of the back of the jeep, his hand, strong and hard, closed for a moment over hers.

"Forgiven me, Fiona?" That edge of a smile, flickering over his face, made him rather hard to resist.

"Of course—if you won't do it again," she said, smiling, too.

"Thanks. I'll try to keep my opinions to myself unless they're strictly flattering. By the way, Colin tells me you're keen on sailing."

"Yes. I love it," she told him eagerly.

"Tomorrow's Sunday, and there'll be the usual racing in the gulf. I own a Snipe. I was wondering if you'd care to crew for me?"

"Oh, I'd love to," Fiona cried. She was wondering why she felt so inordinately pleased. She saw that his eyes held amusement in their steely depths as he waved goodbye. She supposed that, like Oliver, he found her

30

enthusiasm naive. But she didn't mind. She was going sailing with him tomorrow. . . .

On the gallery, Colin was waiting with a bundle of home mail that had arrived that morning.

Fiona and Dawn took their letters and opened them at the luncheon table, reading out bits to each other excitedly.

Suddenly Dawn's cheeks flushed. With an air of being unable to hold back the rush of words she cried, "Colin, here's something mommy says. Listen, darling. You remember her brother, Uncle Reggie, who farms in Dorset?"

"Of course." Colin's eyes had become suddenly wary. He laid down his knife and fork.

"Darling, he says the time has come when he has to take a partner. He—he wants *you*, Colin. He'd be simply delighted if you'd consider it. In your own time, of course—but as mommy says, he's no chicken, and the sooner the better. Oh, Colin, isn't it a wonderful chance? You will, won't you? Please say you will. Mommy tells me . . . ."

But Colin had pushed aside his plate and stood up. His eyes were harder, his expression sterner than Fiona had ever imagined it could be.

"Do we have to go into all this, again, Dawn?" he asked wearily. "Once and for all, my job is here, at Cassia."

He left the room, and they saw his tall figure go striding down the avenue.

"If he loved me half as much as he loves Cassia," Dawn said stormily, "He'd do as I ask, without argument."

Fiona felt she couldn't let that pass unchallenged.

"You know he adores you," she said. "But Cassia has belonged to generations of Murrays. . . ."

"And belongs no longer," Dawn snapped.

"I know, darling, but he still feels the same about it, I expect. Surely, surely you don't expect him to give up his—his lifework, just for a whim of yours!"

"Whim! If that's all you think it is. But I might have known you would side with Colin," Dawn said bitterly.

"My lamb, I'm not siding with anyone. But it just doesn't make sense to me that you should want to throw up all this—your lovely house that's run so beautifully without your lifting a finger, this easy, luxurious life . . . ."

"All that—and a husband who forgets I'm here half the time."

"Rubbish," Fiona told her briskly. "Colin's a very busy man, with big responsibilities. What's eating you, Dawn? You loved it here at first. And you knew, when you married Colin, you'd have to live here."

"But don't you see, I was so terribly in love I'd have followed Colin to—to Timbuktu. And I admit it was rather fun at first, sort of romantic and glamorous. Colin was different then. He used to take me places—and if he couldn't, there was Bill. Bill used to ride and swim with me. But then crop time came around, and I just didn't exist for either of them.

"Even then I didn't mind so much—till Colin's mother got busy telling me all about oil riots and what the rioters did. It was frightful, Fiona. They went crazy and burned people alive. Mamma-in-law kept on prophesying what she calls mischief, saying that what had happened once would probably happen again, till I felt as if I was sitting on the top of a volcano that might erupt any minute. That's why I don't want children till

Colin takes me home. I don't want them if they have to grow up here," Dawn finished desperately.

So that was it. The truth was out. Dawn had lost her nerve, as well as her faith in Colin's love.

She went on passionately. "Honestly, Fiona, I never dreamed Colin could refuse to take me away, once he saw I wasn't happy here. I thought he loved me."

Fiona, torn between exasperation and loving sympathy, gazed at her helplessly, hardly knowing what to say.

She was taken aback when Dawn cried, "Promise to help me, Fiona. Swear that when Colin talks to you about me—as, of course, he will—you'll say you think I ought to go home. Tell him he should leave here and take me. Say I'm ill, anything you like. *Promise.*"

The last thing Fiona wanted to do was give any such promise. But Dawn's excited manner suggested that hysteria wasn't far off. She said hurriedly, "Well, I'll do my best," and then wished she hadn't, for Dawn got up and flung her arms around her. "Oh, I knew you'd get me out of here. Bless you," she almost sobbed.

Later as Colin was driving Fiona to the dispensary, he said curtly, "Look, Fiona, for heaven's sake try to make Dawn understand I can't leave Cassia, will you? She mustn't badger me. She knew I wouldn't get another home leave for four years. She hasn't got all that long to wait, yet she nags and nags. I did hope she'd be more like herself, now you're here."

Miserably she remembered her promise to Dawn. With an effort that took all her courage she said diffidently, "Have you thought . . . could you, perhaps, let her go home . . . ahead of you, I mean? She isn't herself, anyone can see that. Perhaps the climate . . . I

33

mean, she doesn't eat, and all that smoking . . . perhaps a change might . . . ."

"So she's persuaded you, has she? And you back her up? I must say I expected something more realistic from you. Honestly, don't you think she ought to be happy? What more does she want?"

Fiona couldn't say, "She wants your time, your attention, your wholehearted devotion. She wants to have you feel the world—and Cassia—well lost for her. She's jealous of Cassia. And she's scared of the island. She feels there's something sinister under its beauty. Your mother has scared her. . . ."

They were turning into the gateway of the factory compound now. Colin stopped the car and led her to a block of offices. Opening a door bearing the printed notice, Manager, he said equably, "Finished, Bill? Then show Fiona around will you? And then take her along and introduce her to doc."

Bill Derwent, pipe in mouth, had been bending over a desk on which were some blueprints. He said pleasantly enough, "Oh, hello, Fiona. Yes, Colin, of course," but he didn't, she observed, seem in the least overjoyed. In fact there was a distinct frown between his brows as he slid the blueprints together and put them up on a rack.

CHAPTER THREE

For the next half hour, Fiona and Bill picked their careful way among rumbling machinery and gurgling chutes carrying streams of syrup from the crushed canes—all the incomprehensible paraphernalia of a busy sugar factory at crop time. Bill shouted brief explanations of the various processes in her ear, and she nodded brightly to show she understood.

"So now for the clinic and your colleagues to be. We'll go in the jeep," he said as he led her into the fresh air.

The long white building, shiningly modern, was divided into departments for medicine, dental surgery, dispensary and the laboratory for the research staff.

It was evidently child-welfare day in the department with which she was concerned. Outside the door stood a crowd of black women, each with a child on her hip, or a toddler or two hiding behind her wide cotton skirts.

Bill had knocked on an inner door labeled Dr. McElroy. Now a voice, unmistakably Scots, called out, "Yes, who's that? Come in."

A local girl in a white uniform opened the door to them, and as Fiona walked in, Bill told the doctor, "Here's your new dispenser, doc. Miss Fiona Leigh. Fiona, Dr. McElroy. He isn't nearly as fierce as he tries to look."

Dr. McElroy had immensely bushy eyebrows above shrewd light blue eyes. As she held out her hand, smiling rather shyly, he asked, "Leigh? L-e-i-g-h?"

"Yes, doctor."

"There was a man of that name, Raymond he was, in my year at Edinburgh. Would you be any relation?"

"He's my father," cried Fiona, delighted, and Dr. McElroy chuckled.

"And have you worked for him as dispenser?"

"Yes, for four years."

"Well, well. That's fine. We must have a talk later on. Just now I must finish with my wee patients. You'll be wanting to see the dispensary and take a look at the research lab. Do that, and then come back here. We're busier even than usual today—there's a bumper crop of childish ailments this week."

"Then—couldn't I stay and help, doctor? If I can borrow an overall, I'd be delighted to start in right away."

"We-e-ell. D'ye really mean that? My medical stores' keeper has been helping me since Miss Burton decided she preferred matrimony to medicine. Have ye got a spare overall, Emmy? This is Nurse Emmy, Miss Leigh. She's as good as she looks."

The nurse gave a shy giggle. "Yes, sure I can find a clean overall, doctor," she said brightly.

"And I'll take you around the lab myself when we're through," the doctor promised.

"Then if you'll excuse me, Fiona, I'll be off," Bill interposed. "You'll be able to get a lift home?"

"Aye, I'll see to that," said Dr. McElroy. "Fiona, he calls you? A guid Scots name. I've a mind to use it myself if you've no objection—seeing I knew your dad. Come then, to the dispensary, and we'll start you working right away." Opening a door, he waved her into a streamlined chrome-and-enamel room equipped with glass-fronted cupboards and ranks of pull-out drawers.

"Here comes your relief . . . Carlton," he went on,

addressing the tall, thin black man who stood with his back to them at a mahogany pedestal desk that looked oddly out of place. Its lid stood open, and the medical stores' keeper hastily closed and locked it before swinging around and coming forward, with an outstretched hand.

"Carlton Marcel—Miss Leigh," said the doctor. "You'll not be sorry, I'm thinking, to hand over. Just show Miss Leigh where you keep things, and then let her carry on. She's well accustomed to the work."

With a feeling of unreality Fiona took the man's hand. This was none other than the stranger who had scared and bullied poor Cupid yesterday evening. The very last person she would have expected to find in the clinic.

He looked, of course, completely different in his long white coat and the horn-rimmed glasses with tinted lenses that lent him such an earnest, studious air. He didn't show a trace of yesterday's menace and arrogance as he said politely, "Sure, doctor. I can hand over to Miss Leigh right away. Everything is in order."

The doctor said pointedly, "Marcel has charge of all the medical and lab equipment and stores, Miss Leigh. A very responsible job. He'll issue you daily with what you require."

"Thank you, doctor," said Fiona. With an effort she went on pleasantly, "You must have been very busy, doing the dispensing as well as your own work. Will you show me where things are?"

"Sure, a pleasure, Miss Leigh," he agreed formally, going over to the desk again and picking up the bunch of keys he had left there.

Marcel certainly knew his job. He ran through lists of drugs and medicaments, exhibited the contents of the poison cupboard, unlocked drawers to show their neatly arranged contents and explained the system of book entries. No wonder the doctor valued him.

Even so, Fiona was glad when he went off and left her alone. She worked steadily, mixing and bottling and labeling—familiar work that interested her and gave her no trouble.

She enjoyed talking to the mothers when they came in with shy, friendly smiles, to collect their medicines.

"The kids just love anything you give them to swallow, the nastier the better," said Dr. McElroy, coming in to see how she was getting on.

"I love them," she exclaimed as the last one went off. "They're so friendly."

He gave her one of his shrewd glances.

"I'm glad to hear that, Fiona. I was a wee bit worried. Marcel, too—he's sensitive. He's a good man, you know. He'll go far."

Dr. McElroy led the way out into a lobby and through swing glass doors. The sugar-research laboratory had long benches decorated in wildly surrealist patterns of test tubes, flasks, retorts, microscopes and tanks. Over these brooded earnest young scientists in white jackets.

Dr. McElroy said loudly, "Hrrrrm. This is our new dispenser, Miss Fiona Leigh."

At once heads jerked up, and a buzz of greetings broke out. Her guide was rattling off names, but too fast for her to sort them out. Behind his back the young gentlemen of the research staff were blowing her kisses and striking attitudes of stunned admiration, hands clasped as if beseeching her for a date.

One, who had pursed up his lips in a silent wolf whistle, had such a merry, handsome face that she had to smile at him, thinking how very attractive he looked and wondering who he was.

She managed to straighten her face and listen with attention to Dr. McElroy's explanations of plant-disease cultures, sugar-syrup samples and seedling experiments.

They were just preparing to leave for the day when a jeep drew up outside. Bill Derwent jumped out and joined them.

"If Fiona's ready, I'll run her back," he announced casually. "It'll save you a detour, doc."

"Aye, it will," agreed the doctor, giving Bill a look behind which lurked a knowing twinkle. Bill returned it calmly, without a flicker of expression on his poker face.

"Right. Coming, Fiona?"

"Yes, Bill." Her voice was sedate, but her eyes sparkled at him, "It was nice of you to pick me up," she said, as he helped her into the jeep.

"Yes, wasn't it?" he agreed calmly. "Did you have a good afternoon?"

"Splendid. I'm going to love the work there."

"Hmm. Let's hope you won't change your mind. Look, I'm going to make a round of the boundaries to inspect the fireguards. Would you like to come? Afraid the road's a bit rough."

"I don't mind. Are you—expecting cane fires, Bill?"

He shrugged. "In a general way, we always expect them. They're among our occupational hazards, you might say."

"Mrs. Murray told us the field hands were singing the fire song," Fiona said.

"Yes. And I told you someone was trying to raise trouble here at Cassia, didn't I? And that's the form it

39

might take. Strikes, riots, fires—the island has seen them all from time to time. Clever agitators want to stir things up.''

He turned the jeep off the pavement onto the rough earth road and drove around the perimeter of the cane fields.

The daylight was fading, and lights twinkled out from the bungalows and labor lines. Above the noise of the jeep's engine, Fiona could hear a chorus of voices and a pulse of music as they drove past the first line of huts.

"Everyone dances far into the night on Saturdays,'' Bill told her. "Specially a time like this, when Carnival isn't far off.''

"Do they? Most of the workers seem so contented. Have they got any *real* reason to make trouble, Bill?''

He shrugged again. "Not really. They're decently paid and fairly treated. The seasonal workers have a legitimate grouse about their quarters—I showed you those. And the regulars are all het up about the new machinery. They've got the mistaken idea it's going to put them out of work, whereas it's merely going to replace the old outworn stuff, and make for efficiency instead of waste. Somebody's been getting at them, you see, as I said before. Propaganda.''

He pulled up at the first of the fire posts, an earthen tower, raised high above the cane tops so that the man on guard had a clear view over the block in his charge, out of which a head popped like a jack-in-the-box at Bill's hail.

All was quiet, it seemed. No alarms. Admonishing the man to be on the lookout in case of a wind change, Bill pulled out his pipe. He seemed in no hurry to go on.

"There's an electric sort of atmosphere these days,'' he said reflectively, "as if it only needed some little

40

thing to touch off a storm. I noticed it today when we were paying the wages. Generally that's the time for a lot of chaffing and tomfoolery. But there was very little fun today. One gang especially was quiet and sullen. But they," he added with his edge of a smile, "have a special grouse against me just now."

She felt a sharp stab of alarm.

"You? What've *you* done, Bill?"

"Fined them heavily," he told her cheerfully, "at a time when they want every penny they can raise for playing Ole Masque and for the Carnival a week Monday. You see, Fiona, they'd been pinching young trees for firewood. They'd almost stripped a new wooded area we put in for a windbreak two years ago—so now they're having to foot the bill."

"But—but they wouldn't do anything—to you, would they?" Fiona asked anxiously.

He gave her an amused sideways glance that seemed to say, "You funny little thing." Like Colin, it would take a good deal to ruffle him. He started up the jeep again and drove on in silence, punctuated by hails to the guards.

Presently he asked casually. "Well, what did you think of your colleagues at the clinic?"

"I thought the doctor was a pet. And Nurse Emmy, too."

"And that fellow Marcel?"

She hesitated a moment. "I don't think I care for him at all," she said frankly.

"No? Any special reason?"

"We-e-ell . . . ." Impulsively she told him of the incident of Marcel and Cupid. "Don't you think it was rather odd?" she finished.

"Very odd," he said absently.

41

As they drew near to the Great House he said, "You *are* crewing for me, aren't you? Colin is going to come down and see the finish. He loves sailing, but can't spare the time for it as a rule."

"Oh, I know, Bill. Such a pity. He's a wonderful helmsman. I used to sail with him a lot in the Solent. . . ." She stopped, flushing a little. Those weren't days she particularly wanted to think about.

"Did you? That was before he married Dawn?" Bill's voice was oddly gentle. She was sure, then, that he knew that she had once loved Colin. Dawn must have told him.

The strange thing was that she didn't mind his knowing.

They had turned into the jacaranda avenue. Now he pulled up at the foot of the steps. The lamps were lighted on the balcony, where Dawn was lying in a long chair, listening to the radio. She was smoking as usual. Her shoulder-length hair shone like gold silk in the lamplight, and her eyes were very bright—so bright that Fiona guessed she had been crying.

She called out petulantly, "Oh, Fiona, I thought you'd never get back. What on earth kept you so long—" She broke off as Bill joined them, and conjured up a brilliant smile. "Come and pour out some drinks, and amuse us. I've been so unutterably bored."

Bill gave her a level, appraising glance.

"Colin not back yet?" he asked.

"Oh, yes, just. He went straight up to bathe and change. He's been playing with the new machinery. He's like a child with a new toy. His Meccano, I call it." The laugh that followed tinkled unnaturally. Dawn was evidently in one of her moods.

42

Bill began to talk of tomorrow's race, showing no signs of having noticed. "You'll come down and watch, Dawn?"

"Would you like me to? Then I will. I'll bring down a huge picnic lunch and we'll have a party. We'll go swimming afterward," she cried with sudden, brittle-sounding gaiety. "Of course," she added with a meaning laugh, "Fiona will want me to phone Oliver and get him to join us—won't you, my pet?"

"I—oh, yes, of course, if you like," Fiona answered, aware that Bill was watching her with an expression of cynical amusement. Really, it was maddening of Dawn. . . .

She was glad when Colin joined them, bathed, changed into cool whites and, though he still looked strained and tired, in his usual calm good humor.He dropped a light kiss on Dawn's cheek before mixing himself a whiskey and soda and sitting down.

"Well, what's the news?" he began comfortably.

"News? Nothing special. Except that Fiona's put in an afternoon's work at the clinic, and Julie's back home," Bill told him. "Braines brought her over from San Fernando this afternoon."

"Mother and children doing well?"

"Fine and flourishing."

"Julie?" repeated Fiona, mystified.

"My spaniel," Bill explained. "I sent her to the vet for the interesting event—couldn't give the time to looking after her myself, and couldn't leave her to servants. I've missed her badly, though—the only woman in my bachelor establishment."

Fiona smiled at that. She was glad he was a dog man.

"Perhaps you'll all come around to my place for a

43

sundowner tomorrow evening and meet the family. Julie's awfully proud of her quads. She'll love showing them off to you."

This was quite a new side to Bill. Who would ever have imagined he'd be so nicely silly about a dog?

The four of them sat on for a time, Colin and Bill and Fiona chatting in the desultory way of good friends who are not trying to impress one another. Dawn said very little, lying back in her chair, still rather sulky, and lighting one cigarette from another.

Then a motorcycle came tearing up the driveway, ridden by a police sergeant. He stopped his engine and shouted urgently, "Mr. Derwent? Oh, sir, what relief to see you! We were afraid you were dead inside your house. It burning, sir. Come quickly."

Fiona heard Bill say, "My God, Julie," as he leaped down the steps three at a time and wrenched open the door of the jeep.

"Wait, I'm coming, too," Colin shouted, dashing after him.

Fiona and Dawn watched anxiously, then Dawn turned back onto the gallery, saying feverishly, "Oh, God, this ghastly island. Just one thing after another. More mischief, I suppose. Let's go up and change; I don't suppose they'll come back for hours." Her voice was weighted with self-pity.

Without replying, Fiona ran up to her room, showered quickly, and did her face and hair with concentration, so as not to think of all the unpleasant things that could happen to a man inside a burning house.

Not long after she went down, the jeep came back. Colin jumped out, followed by a black-and-tan spaniel, her tail moving anxiously. Then Bill joined them, carrying a large round dog basket. Julie ran beside him,

44

whining a little, as he mounted the steps. Fiona saw that his hands and arms were bandaged.

"Oh, you're hurt, Bill," she cried.

"Nothing much," he told her indifferently, putting the basket down. "I scorched myself a bit, beating out Julie's bedding."

Fiona was down on her knees, exclaiming over the basket's contents. The puppies seemed quite unperturbed. They opened sleepy eyes when she touched their silken coats.

"Your bungalow—what happened, Bill?" asked Dawn.

"Gutted. My boys had managed to get a few things out. But I'm afraid there's precious little left."

"Bill had better settle in here till we can find him new quarters—eh, Dawn?" Colin suggested.

"But of course."

"That's very good of you," Bill said.

"Lord, you're lucky to be alive," Colin told him emphatically. "Another minute and that fall of rafters would have got you—"

Dawn cried out suddenly, hysterically, "Your mother said they were going to start fires. I suppose this is only the first. Oh, God, can't you see, Colin? Why do we stay on here? Why don't we get away while we can?" Then she burst into a storm of tears.

Colin went to her at once and put his arms around her, trying to soothe her. "Dawn, darling, please . . . ."

But she pushed him angrily away. "No, no. Leave me alone. I've begged you a hundred times. But you just won't listen. . . ."

45

CHAPTER FOUR

WHEN HELOISE WOKE HER the next morning, Fiona lay still for a while, with a feeling that something nice was going to happen. Of course—the yacht race. Jumping out of bed, she flung on a flowered housecoat and stepped out onto the gallery to look at the day.

It was perfect—clean blue sky, sunlight pouring like liquid gold over mountains, foothills and plain and the canes rippling like the waters of an inland sea as the fresh trade wind came singing over from the Atlantic. *A lovely sailing breeze,* she thought happily.

Just below her, she could see dozens of tiny hummingbirds already at work, dipping their beaks into the hibiscus flowers. Their feathers gleamed jewellike in the morning light. She watched them entranced; they were too lovely to be true. Suddenly she broke out into a little song of sheer delight. "Oh, what a beautiful morning, Oh, what a beautiful day . . ." and swung around, flushed and laughing, when she heard a pleasing baritone voice.

"I've got a wonderful feeling, Everything's going my way."

"Good morning, Bill," she called—for there he was, farther along the balcony, also inspecting the day.

"Grand sailing wind, Fiona."

"Fine. How are the hands?"

"Not too bad, thanks."

"And the family?"

"I've just been down to see them. They're breakfasting."

"Which is what I'm going to do, any minute now."

With a wave of her hand she vanished into her bedroom, showered, and donned blue denim jeans, a thin, opened-necked shirt and rubber-soled shoes.

Downstairs she found Bill and Colin already dealing with eggs and bacon and kidneys, toast and marmalade, and fragrant coffee. In the middle of the table Cupid had made a beautiful arrangement of oranges, mandarins, a pineapple and bananas, embedded in greenery.

Afterward she and Bill went to see the puppies in the stables.

"Oh, they're adorable," she cried as the little creatures, with silky ears flopping and pink tongues hanging out, wobbled on uncertain legs around the yard.

"They're just a month old. Two weeks more, and they'll be ready to leave home." He started to gather them up and pop them into their basket, while Julie, like an anxious nanny, pushed back the ones that tried to scramble out again.

He added, as if it were very much of an afterthought, "By the way—the three bigger ones are already spoken for, but if you'd like to have the little one . . . ."

Fiona's eyes opened wide.

"You'd give her to *me*? Oh, Bill . . . ." Her delight made her inarticulate. She could only pick up the little bitch puppy and hold it against her face. Her shining eyes met Bill's and for a long moment seemed to hold them. He put out a hand and touched the puppy's head, brushing Fiona's cheek as he did so. She held her breath. But then she felt him withdraw, and the puppy began to wriggle in her arms.

Bill said brusquely, "Why not? I'd been wondering where I could find her a home. You can take her when the others go."

"Thank you, Bill." She felt exactly as if a door had

been shut in her face. She set the puppy down and went off to find Dawn.

She found her on the back gallery, watching Cupid prepare the picnic. The long serving table was loaded with cold guinea fowl, salads, stuffed crab backs, eggs, crisp rolls, cheeses and piles of fruit. There were big thermos bottles of iced coffee, and of the rum punch without which no Trinidad picnic would be considered complete.

"Heavens, what a feast, and how awfully good it looks," she exclaimed.

The butler gave her a complacent look as he deftly wrapped and stowed.

"I'm tellin' you, Miss Fiona, ma'am, this picnic's going to be good," he said. "You go swimming, and sailing on the sea, you'll want plenty of liquor and eats."

"We certainly will," Fiona agreed smiling. "I say, Dawn, did you invite Oliver? Is he joining us?"

"Need you ask?" Dawn wore the triumphant look that sat so ill on her charming face. "He simply jumped at it. He'll be waiting for us at the club. Thank heaven for Oliver. He can always find time to be amusing, bless him."

Fiona let the implied gibe at Colin pass. She said peaceably, "How marvelous to be able to arrange a picnic ahead and know it will be fine. What a climate!"

Dawn lifted her slim shoulders in that small disparaging shrug. "This is our dry season. But wait till the rains start. Sixty-five inches, can you imagine? Such storms, thunder and lightning and torrents of rain. And mud. Thick sticky mud all over the place. You won't rave about the climate then. You'll be too busy slaughtering mosquitoes and flying ants and buzz-bomb beetles and what have you. This sugar belt is the wettest part of the island—it has to be or else. Sugar," she repeated in a voice of detestation.

They found Bill standing beside the station wagon chatting amiably with Cupid. They drove swiftly southward in the drenching sunlight, under a sky whose cerulean blueness was already turning milky with the heat. The countryside had a lush technicolor look, the vegetation was rampant and richly green. It exhaled a hot, tropical smell that Fiona was beginning to recognize and rather like.

The club surprised Fiona by being quite imposing, set in a compound full of flowering shrubs, with tennis and squash courts nearby, and a jetty for boats in front.

"Behold the center of the social and sporting life of Pointe-à-Pierre," Bill said with a wave of his hand. "Not a bad spot. There's a good dance floor."

Fiona found herself wondering what it would be like to dance with Bill. She hadn't, somehow, associated him with anything so frivolous. But she was still smarting too much from the earlier rebuff over the puppy to do more than say politely, "It looks very grand."

As they pulled up at the main portico, Oliver appeared in the doorway, very elegant in well-pressed white flannels, and a white silk shirt with an expensive look. Bill muttered something, but Fiona couldn't catch what he said.

"Hello, Fiona, my sweet," he called as she jumped down from the station wagon. "That's an awfully fetching getup. You look quite enchantingly nautical."

"It's meant to be practical," she said with her fresh young laugh, amused at his unfailing gallantry, but pleased all the same.

With a raucous toot on its horn a long, open sports car came swishing to a halt behind the station wagon, and a young man and woman jumped out. The young man was tall, slim flanked, dark haired and dark eyed. At the sight of Fiona his remarkably handsome face lighted up as if someone had pressed a switch. He came toward her eagerly, smiling and holding out his hand. When Fiona gave him hers, he took and held it as if he couldn't let go.

"I say, hello, good morning, Miss Leigh," he said, his eyes devouring her. "You do remember me, don't you—at the clinic, in the lab, yesterday afternoon?"

Recalling the silent wolf whistle, Fiona said dryly, "Yes, I remember," and reprovingly shook her head.

But the young man was quite unabashed.

"Oh, good. I meant you to," he went on. "I say, are you racing, too? With Bill? That's marvelous, though I warn you we're going to beat you today. Look, you must sail with me in the *Calypso* sometime, will you? Come sailing with me this afternoon after the race," he went on with sweeping enthusiasm, oblivious of everyone but herself. "I'll take you up the gulf as far as the Five Islands, and we'll swim there. Will you come? Please say you will."

"Well, I'm afraid not this afternoon. . . ."

A voice behind her broke in. "Aren't you going to introduce me, Leon?"

"Oh—I'm sorry. This is my sister, Lorraine. Lorraine, Miss Fiona Leigh. Our name is de la Torre."

The girl who looked about nineteen and was perfectly lovely, showed small pearly teeth in the friendliest, gayest smile. "Why, hello, Fiona, my dear," she said in her singsong island voice. "Leon has told me *all* about you."

"Has he? All?" said Fiona, raising her eyebrows.

"Well, plenty," Lorraine assured her laughingly.

The moment she had turned away to greet the rest of

the party, Leon went on urgently. "Then you'll race with me next week, won't you? And Fiona—I may call you Fiona—will you come dancing here on Saturday night? Rather a special, pre-Carnival dance?"

"Well, you know I'm Dawn's guest. I'll have to see what she's doing. . . ."

"Oh, I'll fix that," Leon told her confidently.

I've made a conquest, Fiona thought, amused and rather flattered. *He's attractive and quite wonderfully handsome. Leon de la Torre. Such a romantic-sounding name!*

She glanced away and caught a hard smile of mockery from Bill Derwent. She was furious at feeling her cheeks grow hot.

Lorraine came along and thrust an arm through hers. "I'd better just take Fiona along and show her the change room, Bill," she said, giving him a melting glance. "We're going to have a wet sail today, don't you think?"

Bill nodded briefly.

"Lots of whitecaps outside," Lorraine went on happily, "and you can really get wet sailing Snipes, as I expect you know, my dear?"

Fiona admitted this was so.

"I suppose you know how honored you are, sailing with our star helmsman?" went on the lovely creature vivaciously as they reached the change room. "I'm so jealous I could kill you, my dear. My ideal man. So remote and inscrutable, isn't he—and quite unattainable, alas."

She sighed gustily, as if to indicate unplumbed depths of unrequited passion.

Fiona said lightly, "Is he? I wouldn't know."

"You wouldn't know? But hasn't anyone told you?"

"Told me what?" begged Fiona.

"My dear, he got engaged to a girl, five years ago, and she came here to marry him. But after she'd seen the sort of life Cassia offered, she ran right back to Toronto and the Mountie officer she'd turned down for Bill. He was quite shattered. So now he's signed off marriage for good. Don't fall for him, darling. There's no future in it at all."

"I—why, I hardly know him. I've only been on the island three days." Fiona protested so warmly that Lorraine gave her a shrewd glance.

"It didn't take three *minutes* for Leon to fall quite madly in love with you," she retorted sagely. "But madly, my dear. He suffers from extreme susceptibility, like me, like all the de la Torres. He's crazy, but sweet—like all my family. Be nice to him, darling, please."

She found Bill waiting for her with restrained impatience.

"Sorry, Bill. Lorraine got talking," she said in apology.

To her relief he took this with a grin. "How I know Lorraine when she gets talking! Come on, we'll go aboard. Dawn has gone off somewhere—with that fellow Hayne."

As they walked along the jetty Fiona couldn't resist asking curiously, "Bill, why are you always so—so unfriendly to Oliver? Do you dislike him so much?"

"I dislike philanderers on principle," he told her shortly.

"But—*is* it just philandering? Mightn't he be genuinely in love with Dawn?"

"Colin's wife," Bill retorted with that unpleasant edge to his voice.

"Well, really, Bill," exclaimed Fiona, indignation ousting discretion, "people can't love or not, just to order. It isn't a thing you can help or be logical about."

"You can try," he countered crisply. After a moment he added, giving her an odd, ironical glance. "Hayne is lucky to have such an ardent champion. But women find him irresistible, and you're no exception, it seems."

I asked for that, she thought wryly.

"Don't be absurd," she countered with spirit. "I've only known him on board, but he was sweet to me. I count him among my friends."

He said nothing, but gave her a skeptical look that brought the blood to her cheeks again. Fuming she walked ahead to his dinghy with her nose in the air.

Taking the single oar, he sculled over to where the *Alouette* bobbed friskily at her mooring some fifty yards away. The water was flecked with white foam, and little waves slapped at *Alouette*'s side. The fresh breeze sang through the wire rigging as they stepped aboard.

"Perhaps, we'd better call it peace till after the race, don't you think?" Bill suggested pleasantly.

"All right," agreed Fiona, polite, but by no means effusive. *I wish we didn't bicker so,* she thought crossly. Then resolutely she put everything out of her mind except *Alouette* and the race.

Leon and Lorraine were hoisting their sails not far away. At least a dozen other boats, some of them Snipes, one or two Stars, the rest a mixed bag, were already sailing around testing the set of their sails and the strength of the breeze. It was a sparkling, exhilarating scene, and Fiona absorbed it happily as she helped Bill and listened to his remarks about the course.

When all was ready he told her, "Take the tiller. All set? Then I'm casting off."

He let go the mooring chain and buoy, and in a matter of seconds the sails had filled, and they were off, heeling sharply to the wind, and cutting cleanly through the water with a white mustache at their bows and spray spattering aboard.

Oh, it's grand, it's glorious, it's the loveliest sport in the world, Fiona thought blissfully, handling the little craft with the ease that sailing in the Solent had taught her and happy to see that Bill seemed to have confidence in her skill.

It was exciting as always, jockeying around for position in the brisk breeze and wavy sea, among a crowd of other boats whose crews were just as determined as you were to be over the starting line first.

She began to count the seconds out loud.

". . . seven, six, five, four, three, two, gun," and as the gun fired they were over, a length ahead of Leon's *Calypso*, creaming along in a flurry of foam as they tacked for the first mark.

Soon the bigger boats began to pass them, but that didn't matter, for they were racing on handicap. Fiona saw at once that Bill was a skilled and fearless helmsman who would coax the last half knot out of his craft. She sat holding the jib sheet, keeping a keen eye on their opponents, from time to time giving Bill useful bits of information about the tactics or intentions of this one or the other, and taking her share quietly and deftly in the swift, smooth maneuvers that are the essence and fun of small-yacht racing.

"Good girl," she heard Bill say after a specially neat tack, and a warm glow seemed to suffuse her from head to foot, in spite of the fact that she was pretty wet by now, and thankful for her sweater despite the blazing sun.

She soon saw that the real fight in this race was to be

between *Alouette* and *Calypso*. "I'm beating you today, man, whatever you do," Leon called out defiantly to Bill. Once again Fiona saw Bill's eyelid droop toward her in an unmistakable wink . . . a sardonic sort of wink, as if he were perfectly aware why it mattered so much to Leon to win today.

But on the last leg home the *Alouette* was ahead. As they neared the last mark and prepared to round it to cross the line, Bill murmured contentedly, "Got him now, I think."

She nodded happily, her eyes shining, and made ready to drop the centerboard at his order, while he put up the tiller, hauled the mainsail flat and let it run out on the other side of the mast.

The tricky maneuver was neatly carried out. Fiona felt like whooping with triumph. But she had reckoned without Leon's frantic determination to win at all costs. As the *Alouette* came around to cross the line, he took the crazy risk of trying to cut in between his rival and the home buoy.

Fiona could see the collision coming, but could do nothing to avoid it. The *Calypso* struck her rival amidships and canted her sharply over. The wooden boom swung across again, catching Fiona hard on the side of her head. She gave a little cry and toppled backward into blackness shot with flashes of fire.

Her last recollection was of Bill's furious voice shouting, "Look out, you young fool!"

CHAPTER FIVE

WHEN FIONA CAME TO, she was stretched out on the jetty with a folded coat under her head.

"What happened?" she stammered. "Were we beaten? Was it my fault?"

"Of course not," he said brusquely. "You crewed splendidly."

"But we didn't win?"

"Yes, we did. We crossed the line locked with the *Calypso*, but of course Leon was disqualified for causing the collision. Serves him right, the reckless idiot. How do you feel now? A bit concussed, I'm afraid."

She sat up, a little dizzy, with the beginnings of a thumping headache. "I'm all right," she said rather shakily. "I'm so glad we won, Bill. Poor Leon. Where is he, by the way? Where are the others?"

"I packed them off. They were hovering and offering advice. So I told them to go and get the picnic ready. I'm to take you along if you feel fit enough—if not we'll go straight back to Cassia."

"I'll be all right."

"I've ordered some tea for you and borrowed aspirins. Think you can stand up?"

She nodded, and he took both her hands in his bandaged ones and half lifted her to her feet.

"Ah, here comes your tea."

A club waiter had arrived with a tray. He held it while Bill filled a cup, and Bill's arm was around her waist, supporting her, while she swallowed it. It was strangely sweet to have him taking care of her. If the waiter hadn't been there, she wouldn't have been able to resist putting her head down on his shoulder and bursting into foolish tears.

As it was, she slipped out of his arm as soon as he took her cup from her.

Here I go, she thought ruefully, *on the point of giving my love to a man who doesn't want it.*

Down at the creek they found luncheon already laid out in the shade of a small coconut grove. A chorus of anxious inquiries greeted Fiona, and Leon assiduously arranged her with cushions at her back against a palm trunk.

"Are you going to be fit to stay?" he asked humbly. He was feeling like a murderer, all the more so since the murderee was his latest love. He had already had the rough edge of Bill Derwent's tongue, which he was ready to admit he had richly deserved.

His handsome face brightened when Fiona said kindly, "I wish I could, Leon, but I think I ought to go home and lie down. I'll see you tomorrow at the clinic, I expect. You mustn't worry, please."

"You're an angel," he told her fervently.

As soon as lunch was over, Colin and Bill rose to leave. Leon tenderly helped Fiona to her feet, and held her arm closely as they walked over the sandy ground.

Whether because of her headache, her general feeling of unease at the way her foolish heart was trying again to betray her, or simply the heat, now at its fiercest, the road back didn't seem so glamorous to Fiona as on the outward journey.

At one village close to Cassia, where bunches of green bananas and unripe coconuts hung from strings above the doorways, some sort of celebration was going on. A native band was playing, the rhythm achieved by beating on bottles and tins with sticks and spoons. Men and women were dancing along the roadway in time to it.

All of them seemed rather unwilling to clear off the road to let the cars pass. Not till Bill had called out amiable greetings and tooted on his horn, did they open a way. Fiona thought apprehensively, *This could be difficult.*

"They're getting ready for Carnival," Colin said.

"Working up for trouble, by the looks of it."

"Looks like it . . . ." His face wore a worried look.

She was thankful when they reached the Great House and the cool dimness of its interior.

"You look all in. Better go straight up to bed and have a sleep. If you don't feel better when you wake I'll fetch Doc McElroy to have a look at you," Bill said, looking at her with such concern that she longed again to turn to him and weep away her perplexities in his arms.

But that, she reminded herself, would not amuse Bill Derwent at all. Obediently, without looking at him, she took herself off to her room, lay down in its shuttered dimness, and fell, at length, into an uneasy sleep.

It was dark in her room when she awoke. She switched on her bedside light and saw that it was half-past six. Experimentally she sat up, lowered her feet to the ground and walked across to her dressing table.

The thumping in her head had stopped. She didn't feel sick or dizzy any more. She was paler than usual, and there was a sore place on the side of her head that hurt when she brushed back her hair. Otherwise she seemed to have made a good recovery. She decided to dress and go down for dinner.

Downstairs on the gallery, as she might have expected, she found Oliver, talking softly to Dawn. He got up from his lounge chair as she appeared, and came over to her.

"We were talking over the plans for Carnival next week," he told her.

"Yes, what do you think, Fiona?" exclaimed Dawn, her eyes sparkling. "I had a telephone call just now from Colin's sister, Marjorie. She's invited me to go up to Port of Spain tomorrow and stay till after Carnival."

"You'll go, of course?" Fiona said quickly. "The change will do you good."

Dawn hesitated. "But you've only just arrived, darling. I hardly think . . . ."

"But of course you must go," Fiona urged. "Aren't there all the calypso contests before the actual Carnival? Won't you enjoy those?"

"Yes, one thing I do love is the calypso tents," Dawn admitted. "And I'm fond of Marjorie, and her children are sweet. You're to come up, too, for the big days, Monday and Tuesday. She's invited you—I suppose you'll be working at the clinic up till then?"

"Of course, I shall."

"We've promised to join up with the de la Torre group. You know everybody makes up a party for the big parade of cars and floats. We're going to dress as Hawaiians. I'll fix up your costume and ukulele. Oliver's coming, too, of course. It'll be fun."

NEITHER COLIN NOR BILL seemed particularly delighted to have Oliver's company for dinner although he seemed to lay himself out to be pleasant to the pair of them—and no one could be pleasanter than Oliver or more effortlessly amusing.

But Colin talked of Dawn's impending visit to his sister, and primed Fiona for her first Carnival.

"I'm afraid Bill and I definitely can't join you," he said.

Dawn, catching Oliver's eye, gave her little shrug of the shoulders. Fiona felt sadly disappointed, but cheered up a little when Colin went on.

"I'll run you up tomorrow, Dawn—I ought to say hello to Marjorie. And Bill has some inquiries to make in Port of Spain—he can run Fiona up on Sunday afternoon and come back that night."

"Yes, I'll do that," Bill said agreeably.

Dawn gave him a derisive look and said with deliberate intent to provoke, "Oliver is going up on Sunday morning. Couldn't he take Fiona—to save you the trouble, Bill?"

It was Colin who snapped, "Thanks, Dawn. Bill has to go, anyway. And Fiona will no doubt want to sail in the race next Sunday morning again. Eh, Fiona?"

"Why, yes, provided nobody's going to hit me on the head again," she said with a laugh. The others laughed, too, and the moment of uncomfortable tension passed.

After dinner Bill, who had seated himself next to Fiona for coffee, murmured, "I'm going to see Julie. Like to come and have a word with your child?"

She got up, her foolish heart racing, and went with him across the yard to the stables.

"Look, she knows me already," she cried. She had picked up the little bitch puppy, and it was licking her face eagerly with its pink tongue.

"What will you call her?" Bill wanted to know.

"Sherry," she said without hesitation. "Look at the color of her eyes."

"Pure amontillado," he agreed gravely. "But actually I didn't bring you out here to play with the dogs, Fiona. I wanted to talk to you."

For a moment her foolish heart began to race again. Then she saw his face in the moonlight. There was no suggestion of tenderness in it; in fact it looked rather grim and purposeful. Her heart slowed down to normal again. She listened quietly to what he had to say.

"Something odd happened this morning. Colin happened to want to look at the layout plans for the new machinery in B shed," Bill told her levelly. "And the first thing was, his keys couldn't be found. Cupid swore he'd put them in his trouser pocket as usual, but they just weren't there. He was very worried—that's why he asked me to go back with him. I have a duplicate set, you see. When we unlocked the drawer where he keeps the plans, they were gone. But this evening, when we went back after some searching inquiries led to nothing, the plans were back in their locked drawer again, and the keys were lying on the floor by Colin's desk as if he'd dropped them. If he hadn't chanced to want to look at the plans this morning, nobody would ever have known they'd been tampered with. Well, what do you make of that, my dear Watson?"

Fiona said at once, "I think I saw Marcel last night near the gate. Maybe he had come to get the keys off poor Cupid. I think it smells of sabotage."

"I think so, too. If that machinery were to be destroyed, it'd set back Cassia's finances and progress by about ten years. It'd break Colin's heart."

Horrified she stared into his face. She was surprised to see how calm and confident it looked.

"Listen, Fiona, I want Marcel's fingerprints. I want you to get them for me tomorrow morning at the clinic. You see, I've suspected for some time that Marcel is the chap we're looking for—the one who's behind the disturbance at Cassia."

"You have? What made you suspect him, Bill?"

"This and that. Putting two and two together, it all seems to add up to him. But so far, I've no proof. And I'll need proof to get him deported from the island—and to convince the police and Dr. McElroy, who oddly enough thinks the world of him."

Fiona nodded. "Yes, I noticed that."

"Marcel came here from Jamaica, with excellent recommendations," Bill told her. "But I happen to know he's madly ambitious to get to Europe to train that wonderful voice of his. Which means he'd probably do anything for money. But proof—that's what we want. I have a pal in the police force up in Port of Spain—that's why I want to go up there—to get some inquiries started."

"You said—I'm to get his fingerprints? But, Bill—how?"

Bill's hand came out to stroke Sherry's silky head.

"Well—how about getting him to handle tomorrow's prescription lists? Then bring them to me—and don't mess them up with your own prints. And be very careful not to rouse his suspicions. I have an idea he may be a dangerous sort of customer. Well—can do?"

"I'll try," she said calmly, though actually she didn't like the idea at all. To herself, but, of course, not to Bill, she was ready to admit that she was more than a little afraid of Carlton Marcel.

It rained during the night, and the morning broke crisp and clear, with thin cloud goose-feathering the blue.

Fiona woke early. Her mind leaped at once to the fact that this was Monday morning; she was to start her regular work at the clinic; and she was to get Marcel's fingerprints for Bill.

By eight-fifteen she was downstairs, calling for her

breakfast. She was wearing one of the white medical overalls she had brought with her. Her hair, except for the short crisp curls in front, was coifed in a folded square of starched white muslin. She looked cool and neat and dependable.

Cupid, dapper in freshly laundered whites, wasn't long in bringing her coffee and boiled eggs. But his face wasn't wreathed in its usual smile. He looked harassed and—was it scared?

No wonder, Fiona thought, if he really had been involved in the theft of Colin's keys. She began to speculate on what means Marcel would have to induce Cupid to hand them over. Intimidation? Bribery? It wasn't very pleasant speculation, and she tried to put it out of her mind. She didn't want to believe the dear little man was guilty. . . .

Bill came in while she was pouring her second cup of coffee. He and Colin, she knew, were out every morning by six o'clock, Colin at the factory, Bill seeing his section managers and overseers about the day's tasks in the field. She greeted him with a quick friendly smile.

"Hello, Fiona. Good morning. Feeling all right, I hope?" When she nodded, he went on with a glance of admiring approval that made her heart jerk, "I see you're dressed for the part."

"Yes. This is what I used to wear in daddy's office. I hope you approve, Bill?" she said, then thought how appallingly coy that sounded. Perhaps Bill thought so, too, for his eyebrows went up slightly.

"Can you be ready in five minutes?" he asked presently.

"I'm ready now, Bill," she said softly.

He wasn't talkative as he drove her to the clinic. He seemed in a hurry and drove fast.

She said tentatively, "Thanks for fetching me, Bill."

He answered rather shortly, "No thanks due. Didn't you know that Colin has detailed me to run you to and from the clinic, for the time being?"

"But that's going to be a terrible bind for you," she protested quickly. "Why, you might be out in the cane fields, miles away. I don't think that's a very bright idea of Colin's at all. I can't see any reason why I should need a lift. I can walk—or perhaps there's a bicycle I can use."

"It's much too hot for you to walk in the middle of the day. But I think there *is* a bicycle. Miss Burton used to pedal around on it, and I think I've seen Emmy on it, too. Can you ride one?"

"Of course I can," she told him with a fine scorn. "So you may consider yourself relieved forthwith of your onerous duty."

He grinned and dropped his left hand for a moment to cover hers. Her heart jerked at the unexpected contact.

"Don't underrate yourself, Fiona," he said lightly, giving her hand a friendly squeeze with his hard, warm one before releasing it. "Did I say it was onerous? But I could easily, as you say, be miles away when I'm wanted. I'd like to be sure you have alternative transport—though I fancy some of our young scientists would see to that!"

She glanced at him sideways. His dimple was well in evidence.

"That'd be nice," she retorted with spirit. "So please don't feel you need to be responsible for me."

He looked down for a moment at the clear, candid profile, the curling dark hair under the white kerchief, the firm, rounded chin that was up in the air now as it so often was when he and she had one of their sparring matches.

"You funny little thing," she heard him say softly. At her quick, startled upward glance he jerked his eyes front and kept them there.

When they reached the clinic he said brusquely, "Get those fingerprints as soon as possible, please. I'll call back for you around twelve-thirty. I'm relying on you."

"I'll do my best," Fiona said in a bright, docile manner that made him feel he would like to spank her.

Dr. McElroy was already hard at work seeing the morning's quota of patients. Fiona waved a hand at him and went quietly through into the dispensary. She found Marcel there, standing in his long white coat and tinted glasses at the pedestal desk, which was open. He at once closed and locked it, and they exchanged polite good mornings.

She thought, as she had before, how studious and innocuous he looked. It was odd that, in some way she couldn't define, he suggested menace, too. She had felt it that first time she saw him talking to Cupid. Perhaps it was that his eyes were always hidden?

For something to say she remarked pleasantly, "That desk—it's an attractive piece, an antique, isn't it? How did it get in here, among all this?" she asked, waving a hand at the chrome and enamel around them.

"This desk is mine, my personal property, Miss Leigh," Marcel answered, and she was struck again by the splendid diapason of his voice. No wonder he was ambitious to have it trained. "Do you want that I should move it?" he went on. She could sense a sort of wariness in him, a defensiveness.

She said hastily, "No, of course not."

"Miss Burton gave it to me for a farewell token. She was a good friend to me," he added rather proudly.

Fiona said, "Well, leave it there, it's very handsome." Then she went on carelessly, "I'll come back with the prescriptions as soon as Dr. McElroy has them ready. Will you be somewhere around?''

"Sure, Miss Leigh. I have some checking to do in the store, but I'll be back at ten-thirty.''

She nodded, and passed through into the office, where she busied herself helping Nurse Emmy until the doctor was through, and ready to go off on his rounds.

When she had made up her prescription list, she went back to her own department and sat down to study it, handling it as little as possible. When Marcel came in she held it out to him; "Here you are. Just the usual things—nothing out of the ordinary today,'' she said.

He took it and stood looking through it. She saw with satisfaction that he held it with both hands.

He said quietly, "I'll have everything for you in a few minutes, Miss Leigh,'' and began opening cupboards and drawers and taking out the ingredients she needed.

"I think that is everything,'' he said at last, and laid the list beside her on the bench, weighting it down with a paper knife so that it wouldn't blow away.

It was as simple as that. Why, then, did she feel so strongly that Marcel knew just what she was after—and might just as well have uttered a derisive ha-ha? Pure imagination on her part, of course.

She worked steadily, with ease and accuracy and enjoyment, till eleven o'clock when a clinic worker brought her a tray with tea, milk and sugar. It was followed almost immediately by Leon, in his white laboratory coat.

"My dear, are you all right again?'' he asked in the attractive singsong that was so like Lorraine's, taking both her hands and gazing ardently into her eyes. "I couldn't sleep a wink last night for worrying about you, Fiona. I just can't forgive myself.''

66

She freed her hands and said cheerfully, "I'm fine, thanks, Leon. Just a small bump, that's all. No other evidence of the crime."

"Such a relief, darling. I've been trying to get away to see you all the morning, but I couldn't manage it till now."

She ignored the darling and said matter-of-factly, "Well, find a cup, and you can share my tea."

When he came back with a cup and saucer, he said eagerly, "Saturday will be my sister's birthday—not Lorraine, but Celeste. Did you know I have three of them to plague me? Mama wants to have a dinner party before the dance, fourteen of us if you and Dawn, Bill and Colin will join us. It will be amusing, I think."

"Oh—it sounds lovely. But Dawn is off today to stay with Colin's sister till after Carnival."

"But we absolutely must have Dawn," stated Leon, a young man who, as the idol of his parents and three sisters, was accustomed to having his own way. "I shall drive up and fetch her, and she can return with Lorraine and me on Sunday. I'll telephone Marjorie and fix it."

"You'd better ask Dawn first."

"Of course, my dear. I shall tell her I promised Oliver she would be at the party."

He grinned rather knowingly at that, and Fiona gave him a severe look.

She turned back to her work and busied herself with making up, handing out and listing her prescriptions in her record book. Then Dr. McElroy returned from his rounds.

"Getting along all right, Fiona, my dear?" he asked.

"Fine, thank you, doctor," she assured him.

"Ah, here's your transport," said the doctor, a twinkle in the eyes under the bushy brows. "Very assiduous."

Fiona shot back into the dispensary, carefully picking up the list and brought it out to Bill.

"There you are, it was too easy," she told him, rather proud of herself.

"Good work," he said. "But I'm afraid it's wasted." And he handed it back to her.

"Oh—why, Bill?"

"No fingerprints at all on the keys or the plans—except Colin's and mine. Whoever took them had the sense to wear gloves, it seems."

"Oh, Bill! But you still think it was Marcel?"

"I do. It fits in with my general conception of his activities. But we still haven't got the proof necessary to get him deported. Sacking him's no use—he can still carry on the dirty work. I want him off the island. But at present we've got nothing against him except my hunch—and yours. The police had his quarters searched—nothing! The next thing is to get at his correspondence. He gets an unusual amount—instructions, no doubt—all addressed to him at the clinic. Any idea where he keeps it, Fiona?"

She said in a bewildered voice, "I? No, how would I have?"

"Well, that's what I want you to find out for me."

Suddenly into her mind flashed the thought of the pedestal desk that Marcel kept so carefully locked. If she could get hold of his keys and take a look at the contents of that . . . .

She told Bill about it, and he agreed that it sounded like a good bet.

"All right, I'll try it," she said gamely.

"Look out he doesn't suspect what you're up to," Bill warned her. The words sent a little thrill of alarm tingling through her.

While they were all at lunch Leon telephoned. Dawn

went to take the call and was soon back again, full of the invitation to the de la Torreses' dinner party and the club dance.

"They have a lovely old house—another Great House, Fiona—and the best chef on the island," Colin said. "You'll enjoy it—it's an experience, dinner at La Rochelle. Did you give them my regrets and include me out, too, Dawn?"

"Too? What do you mean? Aren't you going? I certainly am. Leon is going to drive up and fetch me," Dawn said rather defiantly. "And Marjorie knows all about it—Leon phoned her. So you needn't fuss about that."

"I see. Well, sorry I can't be there," Colin said shortly. "As things are now, I prefer to stay on the spot." Fiona saw his glance meet Bill's.

"You go. I'll stay," Bill offered at once; but Colin wouldn't have that. Dawn's expression said plainly that she couldn't have cared less. . . .

She kissed Fiona affectionately at parting and said gaily, "Oh, by the way, I nearly forgot, Leon wants to take you swimming at the creek. He'll pick you up at the clinic at five."

Fiona glanced at Bill and saw that hard mockery in his eyes. She said promptly, "Lovely, I'll get my swim things. I won't be a second, Bill."

"Good, I've no time to spare," he said coolly. He drove to the clinic with his foot hard down, presenting to her a profile so unforthcoming that she didn't say a word, except to thank him rather dryly when they got there safely.

The afternoon was a busy one, women patients again, and a long list of medicines and tablets to make up at the end of it.

It was specially delightful, afterward, to drive in

Leon's sports car in the cool of late afternoon, with the breeze whipping through her hair. It was even nicer floating in the cool water of the creek, watching the pelicans sailing overhead.

Leon was a wonderful swimmer, and they raced each other out beyond the mouth of the creek, then came back slowly, and lay on the sand for a while, watching the sun setting in splendor over the gulf.

Leon said softly, "You know I've fallen in love with you, Fiona darling?"

"Why, Leon, you hardly know me yet," she objected.

"Enough to know how wonderful you are."

She jumped to her feet at that and ran over to the clump of palms where she had left her clothes.

"It's time to go, Leon," she called. "I have to attend to the housekeeping now that Dawn's away." She didn't have to, of course, but it was the best excuse she could think of on the spur of the moment.

CHAPTER SIX

ALTHOUGH IT HAD SEEMED to Fiona that to get hold of Marcel's keys without his suspecting might prove an impossible task, the chance came surprisingly quickly, and Fiona was quick-witted enough to seize it.

On Thursday, just as Marcel had issued her with what she needed and locked up again, Dr. McElroy hurried in and told his assistant he wanted him to come out with him on an urgent case. Marcel said, "Sure, doctor," pocketed his keys and followed the doctor out to his car.

As she heard the engine starting up, inspiration came to Fiona. She ran outside, calling "Wait a minute, please."

"Can't it wait till we've come back?" demanded the doctor.

"I'm afraid I've spilled the magnesia powder. Give me the keys, will you please, and I'll get some more," she said, holding out her hand.

She could see that Marcel didn't like it, but the doctor's bushy brows were bent on him fiercely. Reluctantly he pulled out his keys and started fumbling with them, trying to detach the one she would require. He didn't intend to give her the whole bunch, she thought with dismay.

But the doctor, really incensed by now, saved the situation again by putting the car into gear and letting in the clutch. Fiona made a grab at the bunch of keys as Marcel was jerked back in his seat.

"Thank you," she shouted as the car drove off.

Her heart was beating as guiltily as if she was robbing

a safe. She whisked over to the door leading to the doctor's office and locked it, then she went, shaking with nerves, to the desk.

There was a number of leaflets—but they proved nothing, for they might have been handed on to him by someone else—and pushed away at the back, a big packet of long envelopes held together by a rubber band.

Quickly she did as Bill had told her to do with any letters she might find—took out the contents, slipped in the same number of blank pages and replaced the whole as nearly as possible where she had found them.

She didn't look at the letters herself. That was Bill's business. She simply thrust the sheets into her handbag, then she relocked the desk and unlocked the door. After washing the magnesia powder Marcel had issued her down the sink, she took an equal amount out of the supply cupboard, in case he made a check. Then she replaced the keys on the pedestal desk, and sat down at her own bench to regain her breath and her poise.

Her tea arrived soon after, followed almost at once by Leon. She let him tell her all about the plans for Saturday night without interruption. By the time he had finished, and it was time for him to go back to the lab, she felt almost normal again.

Presently Marcel came back. "There are your keys, all quite safe," Fiona told him pleasantly.

He turned and looked at her for what, in the nervous state his presence seemed to induce, seemed an uncomfortably long time.

"I hope you found what you wanted, Miss Leigh," he said. At that moment, she would have given a lot to see the eyes behind the dark glasses.

He had a long envelope in one hand; evidently the mail was in. He unlocked the desk, opened it and put the envelope inside. Fiona held her breath as he stood staring for a moment or two into the desk. Then he closed it softly, and with a queer formal bow, he left the room.

She felt suddenly far less confident. "Jitters again," she muttered, but the feeling persisted. She was thankful when Bill appeared to run her home for lunch, and she could give him the papers in her handbag.

He seemed so pleased with her success that she decided not to mention her qualms.

On the way back, after lunch, he had disappointing news for her, however.

"I took a look at those letters. They're all from Jamaica—and in some sort of code! It looks as if they're what we're after, but the code has to be cracked before we shall know. Luckily my police pal up in Port of Spain is expert at cracking codes. I'm sending them up to him. Perhaps by Sunday he'll be able to tell us what they're all about. Don't look so downcast, Fiona. You did splendidly. Was it very hair-raising?"

She told him how easy, really, it had been. She also confessed to her odd feeling that somehow Marcel knew. Bill didn't pooh-pooh as she had been afraid he might.

"If we're on the right track," he said seriously, "Marcel must live in a perpetual state of fear of being found out."

She soon had cause to believe that she had been right in sensing menace in Carlton Marcel.

THE NEXT MORNING Leon came in again to share her eleven-o'clock tea. Evidently he intended to make it a habit, and she wondered if she was wise to allow it, and how she could stop it without hurting his feelings.

She handed him his tea with a smile, saying, "Sorry

73

we're short on sugar this morning, Leon. I've split what was left between us," and laughed when he paid her the inevitable compliment about not needing sugar when *she* was there to pour his tea. . . .

Later she pedaled back happily to the Great House on the clinic bicycle, which had been produced and cleaned up for her benefit, and found that Cupid had laid a delicious-looking lunch for one on a small table in a shaded corner of the gallery.

But somehow she had no appetite today. She sat at the table with a book propped against the water jug, reading and trying to eat; but very soon she realized that she was feeling seriously unwell. She kept having stabs of pain, and beads of cold sweat broke out on her forehead. She left the table and went up to the bathroom, mixed herself a big tumblerful of bicarbonate, drank it down and went to lie on her bed.

After a while she was violently sick. The pain ceased then, and she began to feel better, though too weak in the knees to cycle back to the clinic. She decided to try and sleep for a while, then see how she felt. She set her alarm for half-past two, lay for a time vaguely wondering what had upset her and finally slept.

When the alarm woke her she got up and walked around experimentally, finally deciding that she could just manage to make the ride. The sun seemed far hotter than she had known it so far, the light more dazzling, the distance longer. She made it, however, and settled down to her work. She had promised to play tennis with Leon that evening at the club, but was doubtful if she would feel up to it, though she certainly felt better now.

She was called to the telephone later on. Lorraine's charming singsong hailed her.

"Hello, Fiona, my dear. Leon asked me to call you.

It's about our tennis, we were having a foursome, darling. Well, the poor sweet is sick . . . he's had to go to bed. Some sort of food poisoning, we think. He sent his love and a million regrets.''

"Oh, I'm so sorry. Tell him I'll call this evening to see how he is,'' Fiona said.

"Okay, darling. Be seeing you on Saturday.''

Fiona stood for a minute with the receiver in her hand, staring at it in shock. When she went back to the dispensary she looked at Marcel, who was putting fresh stocks of drugs into a cupboard, with something like horror.

She was quite sure that the sickness of both Leon and herself had been no coincidence. They had shared the sugar—the one spoonful that had been left in the bowl that morning. She remembered now that she had thought the tea rather unpleasant—in fact she had said laughingly to Leon, "Isn't it odd how nobody can make decent tea except oneself?''

Now she was thinking baldly, *No one has access to the poison cupboard except Marcel*. Marcel had tried to poison her—it hadn't been her fancy that he suspected her—Bill had been right when he had said he might prove to be a dangerous customer.

He had his back to her now as he worked at the cupboard. For a moment she felt as if she must get up and run out of the room; she couldn't bear to stay there with him a minute longer.

Then she got a grip on herself. It would do no good to let him know she suspected him. The thought struck her that perhaps he had not expected to see her there. If she had swallowed all the sugar, instead of sharing it with Leon, perhaps she wouldn't have been.

Surely, though, he wouldn't have risked a fatal dose.

That would have meant a postmortem, detectives searching for the truth—the very sort of publicity Marcel would want to avoid.

It was far more likely that what he had intended to do was to warn her; he would know that she understood enough about symptoms to suspect she had been poisoned, and that she was well aware who had the key to the poison cupboard.

The more she thought about it, the more certain she was that the dose she had swallowed had been a kind of keep-off notice.

She didn't see Bill till just before sundown. She was in the garden, sitting on the grass with the puppies gambolling around her, and Julie in anxious attendance.

"Hi, Bill," she called. "I hope you don't mind—I let them out as I didn't know how late you'd be."

"We had a long session in Brighton," he told her. "Just got back. Have you had a good day?"

"Well—if you can just spare a minute, Bill, I'll tell you about it." And it all came tumbling out.

She was quite taken aback by the way Bill received her news. It gave her a thrill of wonder and delight to see how shaken he was at hearing of the risk he had caused her to run. He had both hands on her shoulders, gripping her, almost shaking her, as he demanded tensely, "You're all right now? Sure? You wouldn't like doc to see you? God, how could I have been such a criminal fool as not to expect something like this."

"Oh, but why should you? And I'm perfectly all right, so don't blame yourself, please, Bill," she pleaded, while his hands still held her, and her heart sang, *He must care a little, or he wouldn't feel it so much.*

"I do blame myself," he said. "I'll have to think what to do now, to make sure nothing else of the sort happens. Poor Fiona!"

"Poor Leon," she amended, laughing so as not to betray the tumult of emotion his touch aroused in her. His hands dropped from her shoulders.

"Yes, that was bad luck for him," he said briefly. "Well, thank God no real harm was done. I'll see you don't run any more risks, I promise you. Excuse me now."

And he strode away, leaving her bewildered once again at his sudden change of tone. Had that determination of his that no woman should reach his heart again reasserted itself, cautioning him to look out, not to slip? *I'll never understand him,* she told herself despairingly.

The next morning Marcel was not at the clinic.

"In view of the extra work he's done, I've given him a long weekend off. He'll be back after Carnival," Dr. McElroy explained without a flicker of expression. Fiona wondered just how much Bill had told him.

She said carelessly, "I know where things are now, doctor. I'll manage."

Later in the day, Bill told her that his police friend would see that Marcel was carefully watched in the capital. Meantime, the codes were proving hard to crack. "But he'll do it," he added confidently. "He's never been beaten yet. The only thing is—it's got to be soon."

ON SATURDAY, soon after tea, Leon appeared at the Great House with Dawn, who had decided she preferred to dress for the dance at her own home.

She was in wildly gay spirits, having had a wonderful time in Port of Spain—a cocktail party at Government House, a dance at the country club, and swimming and sunbathing at Maracas Bay and Blanchisseuse.

She had brought with her a box of the lilac-colored Vanda orchids that grew in a great clump in Marjorie's garden. She and Fiona set to work to make themselves corsages such as it is the charming custom to wear at any dance in Trinidad.

"I'm wearing my pale orchid net," Dawn said. "What about you, Fiona?"

"The rose pink, I think. It'll go well with yours."

They began dressing early, running excitedly to and fro between each other's bedrooms. Then they closeted themselves in Fiona's room for the final touches.

"You look perfectly beautiful," Fiona cried generously when they were ready.

"Pretty good yourself, too, my pet," Dawn answered, admiring her own ravishing reflection in Fiona's mirror. She had tucked an orchid into the front of her bodice and had fastened another in her honey-gold hair. Around her neck she wore a chain of amber topaz, the exact color of her eyes.

Fiona's dress had a tiered skirt and a low neckline that showed off her pretty shoulders. She wore delicate flower earrings and a bracelet to match, that Dawn had given her for her twenty-first birthday. Her hair was brushed up at the back into a cluster of curls into which an orchid was tucked.

"Come along, pet, Bill has just gone downstairs. Let's make an entrance," cried Dawn.

Bill was standing with Colin near the foot of the staircase. He wore tails—for the pre-Carnival dance was a gala occasion—and looked extremely well in them.

He and Colin both looked up as the girls walked down the stairs. Both their faces expressed unstinted admiration. Compliments flowed as the two girls sipped their glasses of champagne—for Colin had decided that the occasion demanded something special.

"Oh, Colin, I do wish you were coming," Fiona said warmly, smiling at him over the rim of the glass.

"Me, too," he answered.

Even Dawn said sweetly, "Yes, it's too bad. Couldn't you change your mind, darling?"

"I'm afraid not, my love, much as I'd like to."

"Then you must be with us in the spirit, as doc would say," Dawn rejoined lightly.

They chatted companionably for a few minutes.

"Time to go," Bill said at length.

As usual, Fiona found herself sitting in the back, but she was too happy to care. The look of almost stunned admiration Bill had given her as she came down the staircase had set her spirits soaring and her heart beating a mad tattoo.

As it was though, Leon monopolized Fiona at the dance to such an extent that he quite spoiled the evening for her. She liked Leon, but she would have preferred to meet more of his friends. Bill asked her to dance at one point, but Leon whisked her away a moment later. And for the rest of the evening she couldn't see Bill anywhere. It wasn't until the last waltz that Bill turned up, with Lorraine hanging starry-eyed on his arm. He didn't look once at Fiona, and though she was talking gaily enough to Solange and Cyrille, two of Leon's friends, she felt sad and sorry. The evening had had its wonderful highlights, but quite a lot of disappointment, too.

Bill drove them back very fast to Cassia.

Dawn, sitting in the front with him, was evidently too sleepy to talk. Her head drooped till it rested on his shoulder. Was she asleep—or just being provocative with him as usual?

In the villages, there were still a few revelers around, but most of the cabins were in darkness. Nearer to Cassia, however, a steady thrum-thrumming could be heard above the frog noises and the purr of first gear.

"Oh, look, Bill—fires!" Fiona exclaimed. She had caught sight of them flickering, red and yellow against the distant shadowy darkness.

"Bonfires over in the seasonal workers' lines," Bill said presently over his shoulder. "They'll be dancing and junketing later than ever tonight. Getting themselves worked up into the right mood for Monday. Don't be alarmed; it's all right, I expect."

As they turned in toward the Great House, the noise sorted itself out into drumming and ping-pinging of African zithers and singing.

When they reached the house they found Colin still up and dressed, on the gallery. He had a thermos of coffee and some chicken sandwiches for them.

"Sweet of you, darling," said Dawn, only half-awake.

"Don't thank me," he said, smiling fondly at her. "Thank Cupid. He did all this half an hour ago."

"But—what was he doing up and around at this hour? And you—you're dressed. Haven't you been to bed, Colin?" Dawn asked with a sudden tenseness in her voice. She was fully awake now, staring at Colin with wide scared eyes. "Something has happened, hasn't it? What was it?"

"Trouble?" Bill asked casually.

"Nothing much. They were lighting bonfires and having a torch procession, and some humorist started ringing the fire bell. That brought out a bunch of the fireguards, and when they found they'd been hoaxed there was a bit of a dustup. Nobody badly hurt—a few cuts and bruises and torch burns. No use being too hard on them. Carnival's started already for the workers—we won't get any sense out of them till it's over."

Dawn was staring at him strangely. She had begun to shiver

"Drink up your coffee, darling, and then off to bed with you," Colin told her. "You're chilled and over-tired—and no wonder, arriving home with the milk," he added with a laugh. "It was a pretty good party, I gather."

"Pretty good," Bill agreed.

"And La Rochelle was wonderful," Fiona added.

"Didn't I tell you? The de la Torres have been lucky, hanging onto their land, and of course they made a for-tune in the first world war."

Colin spoke matter-of-factly, without bitterness, but Fiona knew how deep the loss of Cassia affected him; how Cassia still had his devotion and loyalty, though it no longer belonged to the Murrays. If only Dawn would understand. . . .

As was her Sunday-morning habit, Mrs. Murray dropped in at the Great House on her way back from early church service. She stared at Dawn in astonishment and showed frank disapproval when it was explained why she was back home. Colin hastily changed the subject by asking her if the noise and turmoil during the night had disturbed her.

"It certainly did, son," the old lady said grimly. "It's a wonder we weren't all burned to cinders in our beds, with all that business of bonfires and torches. Ah, well, I guessed we'd have trouble this Shrovetide, and I make no doubt I'll be proven right."

"Oh, come, mother," Colin expostulated cheerfully.

"I caught my gardener singing the fire song again," Mrs. Murray went on, with a glance of her needle-sharp eyes at Dawn. "Better see to your fireguards, my boy, for the next few days."

"We always see to our fireguards, mother," Colin

reminded her gently. "Bill has had them trebled this week."

Mrs. Murray snorted, and began to hum the song in her rather harsh old voice.

Fire in da mountain . . .
Nobody foh out him.
Poor John—nobody foh out him.

"But what does it mean?" Fiona asked, for she couldn't make head or tail of the words.

"It says nobody's going to help put out the fire for poor John the plantation manager, my dear."

Dawn jumped up from her chair.

"Oh, let's stop talking about fire, please," she cried frantically. "I hate fire. I'm terrified of it. Why must we always talk about it?"

Mrs. Murray finished her breakfast in ominous silence, in spite of the efforts of Colin, Fiona and Bill to placate her. Even when Dawn said contritely, "I'm sorry, mother, please forgive me," she didn't really soften. She gave Dawn a few messages for Marjorie, and rather royally took her leave.

Bill's left eye drooped toward Fiona in the now familiar suspicion of a wink.

He admired Mrs. Murray tremendously, she knew, but evidently he wasn't prepared to accord quite the deferential, serious respect to her tantrums that Colin gave them.

Fiona admired the indomitable old lady herself—she couldn't help it, but she wondered how she would have felt about her had she been in Dawn's shoes. Poor Dawn, always in her black books. . . .

Oliver was the next visitor. He dropped in, very

elegant in a suit of some light gray material and a beautiful shirt and tie, on his way to Port of Spain. It was decided that Fiona and Dawn should drive on with him—rather to Fiona's dismay, for she would rather have waited until Bill had finished his day's work and could take her.

As it happened, though, Dawn wasn't feeling well and decided to rest for a while after Colin had offered to drive her back to his sister's house later that afternoon.

Fiona didn't have a chance to speak to Bill alone, for he and Colin hurried back to the factory as soon as they had drunk their tea.

But after all, Fiona enjoyed the drive up with Oliver. It was another perfect day. As they left the Great House the air seemed brimful of sound and scent—sound of bird song, of the trickle of the fountain into the lily pond, of the trade wind rustling the palm tops; scent of jasmine and honeysuckle and tuberose, gardenia and oleander, heady and exotic.

Oliver gave her a quizzical sideways glance as he turned the car into the main road.

"This isn't just exactly what you wanted, my pet, is it?" he asked lightly, but with an understanding smile.

Fiona flushed. She said quickly, "Of course. It's sweet of you to take me to town, Oliver."

"But it would have been sweeter to go with Derwent? Don't mind me, I seldom take umbrage. . . . But tell me, my sweet—is this The Real Thing?"

She didn't pretend not to understand. And something moved her to confide in Oliver.

"I—I think it is," she said. "Though how does one really know? Three years ago I thought I would die because Colin loved Dawn instead of me. But now—well, the feelings I had for him seem so tame compared with how I feel about Bill." She stopped short, then went on shyly, "I don't know why I'm telling you about this . . . boring you. . . ."

"Not boring me," Oliver assured her gently.

"Have you ever been in love, Oliver?"

"Hundreds of times," he told her cheerfully.

"No, but I mean really—seriously?"

"One is usually serious about love at the time, my sweet. But if you mean matrimonially, frankly, I'm a bachelor—and like it. At some stage in any love affair," he went on pensively, "I get around to assessing just what I should have to give up, in comfort and independence and mobility, for the doubtful pleasure of the company of one woman for the rest of my life—and, frankly, my ardor wanes. I hasten, before it is too late, to fresh woods and pastures new."

Fiona's clear young laugh pealed out. "Oh, Oliver, you unprincipled philanderer," she cried reproachfully. "You're all wrong, I'm sure. But you do make out a good case for yourself."

THE HOTEL was filled with a lively, chattering throng. Oliver had reserved a table under a vine-clad pergola. During lunch he told her that he would be flying back to London at the end of the week.

"But you're coming back?"

"Unlikely. Unless any more snags develop on the job here. But I don't expect that."

"Oh, Oliver, we shall miss you terribly," cried Fiona. What about Dawn, she was thinking. Dawn would be miserable—but mightn't it be a good thing for her, in the end, if Oliver, with his charm and gallantry and his inspired way with women, were no longer at hand to be compared all the time with Colin? Dawn would get over it.

84

After they had had a long gossip over their coffee, Oliver drove her to Marjorie's house, a pretty bungalow surrounded by a garden full of flowers and shady trees and lawns.

The two older children were playing ball on the grass when they arrived, and rushed off shouting, "Mommy, mommy, people!"

Marjorie was older than Colin, but very like him, with his blue eyes, a touch of gray in her sandy-fair hair, and none of Mrs. Murray's sharpness and censoriousness.

She kissed Fiona with a kindly, "I'm delighted to have you come and stay, my dear. Colin has often talked of you."

Oliver drove back to his hotel for a siesta, and presently Colin and Dawn arrived. But though Marjorie pressed Colin to say, he was in a hurry to get back to Cassia.

Fiona was happy later when Bill telephoned her. "I thought you'd like a progress report, my dear Watson," said his voice over the line, rather indistinctly. "No luck yet with the code. But the police think they've got something else on our friend. If it comes off he'll be deported right away."

"Oh—what, Bill?"

"I can't tell you over the phone. If anything happens, it'll probably be on Wednesday night, so possess your soul in patience. And enjoy yourself, Fiona."

"Thanks, Bill. I will."

CHAPTER SEVEN

ON THE MONDAY that started off the three-day fiesta, every footpath and track and road on the island led in one direction—to Port of Spain.

Pedestrians and cyclists streamed endlessly into the city, buses and trucks and donkey carts decanted their loads, and the little train from San Fernando in the oil region chuffed back and forth, adding its noisy quota to the throng.

All day the hilarious crowds milled in the narrow parallel streets, packed Marine Square and the green savanna, spilled over the quays and into the wider streets of the suburbs and esplanade.

For this was Carnival, the highlight of the year, the panacea for all the sorrows and frustrations of everyday life. This was the time when unreality stepped in, fantasy ruled, and nothing counted but fun, fun, fun. . . .

Fiona and Dawn spent the day with the de la Torre party, picnicking on a smooth golden beach at Toco, at the northeastern point of the island.

That night, after dinner at a Chinese restaurant, the party went out into the town to join the milling throng for a time, and see the lights and decorations. Then they made for the calypso tent of Leon's choice and sat squeezed together among the others on hard wooden seats in the front row.

Leon was in his element here. He was a genuine fan, and knew most of the calypso singers as well as their songs.

"When I was a kid I used to save all my pocket money

to come up and listen to Lion and Lord Pretender, and Lord Radio 'wid de bright glass eye,' Attila the Hun, who was the clever, politically minded one, and Lord Radio 'wid mout' like waterspout.' They were the idols of the people, I can tell you. Some had made their first trip to the States and had received a wonderful reception,'' Leon told Fiona, sitting very close to her, his hand holding hers on the bench between them.

Listening she found the words hard to follow. Many were local French *patois* words; others were oddly accented to achieve the clever two or three-syllabled rhymes beloved of the calypso singers.

But the rhythms were extraordinarily catchy, though unfamiliar. She found she couldn't help tapping her foot and swaying her shoulders, just like everybody else.

Leon was delighted by her enjoyment; the calypsos had been a part of his life as long as he could remember. He wanted her to learn to love everything about this island which to him—as to Colin—was home.

Now Tuesday, the Mardi Gras, the climax of Carnival, dawned hot and dazzlingly bright.

Fiona yawned herself awake in Marjorie's guest room just before ten o'clock, and leaned over to the other bed to shake Dawn by the shoulder.

''Wake up, wake up, you bacchanal,'' she cried, laughing.

By the time they had dressed and breakfasted Leon was there, waiting to take them to his cousins' house on the east side of the savanna, where the de la Torres were staying.

The float they were to ride on was massed with hibiscus blossoms—a handsome setting for the cluster of pretty girls and fine young men. Fiona surrendered like everyone else to the madness that was in the very air.

The hot sun blazed down, the trade winds blew softly, the scent of the flowering trees filled the air, and the spirit of Carnival capered extravagantly among the revelers as they laughed and sang and pelted each other and the crowds lining the route with flowers and confetti.

Leon was at the wheel of the float, with Fiona beside him. As she sank back panting after a prolonged round of the confetti battle, he asked her, "Are you really enjoying it, Fiona?"

"Need you ask?" she answered, trying to smooth her wildly disarrayed curls with her hands.

"Leave them like that, darling, they look wonderful," Leon said softly. His eyes caressed her, and she felt her color deepen.

She wished she could be in love with him as he was with her. Why couldn't she? He was much nearer her own age than Bill—he had a charm and naturalness all his own—he was manly as well as handsome—he was amusing and gentle and sweet. He was intelligent—his job showed that—and he was the heir to La Rochelle.

Why couldn't she love him, instead of making herself miserable over Bill Derwent?

They danced that night at the country club, in an open-sided ballroom that overlooked gardens with crazy paved walks. Fiona walked with Leon in the moon-silvered garden between dances. He deliberately steered her toward the shadows beneath the wide-spreading saman trees.

Suddenly he turned and took her in his arms. They felt strong and hard, like his body. There was warm pleasure in the feel of his lips as she allowed them to press down for a moment on hers. But there was none of that responsive thrill, that fluttering of gossamer wings inside her, that the nearness of Bill Derwent could produce without his even touching her. This was lovemaking, sweet and gently passionate—but for Fiona, it wasn't love.

She put her hands against Leon's shoulders and held herself away from him.

"Please, Leon, no," she begged.

"Darling, why not? I adore you. I want to marry you," he protested ardently. "I've told mama and papa, and all our friends."

She hadn't the heart to give him a blunt refusal. She said, hedging, "I like you very much, and I like your family, too. But please don't ask me to say I love you, yet. That's an awfully big thing for a woman, you see."

Leon looked down at her adoringly.

"Of course, darling. But you see, I'm very impetuous. And I know what I want, and I have to have it when I want it. You mustn't make me wait too long. You'll say yes soon—won't you?"

The only thing that would really have convinced him would have been to say, "I'm in love with somebody else, Leon." And she couldn't bring herself to confess that.

So she let him kiss her again, and wished hard, as he held her, that she could fall out of love with Bill Derwent, and be free to love Leon. That would be the best possible thing for her—if only her foolish heart would behave itself. . . .

Carnival went its undiminished way. The culminating event was the ball at the Princes' Building on Wednesday evening, and while they were there Leon's friends decided to go on to a new nightclub of which two of them were members.

"There a new *chanteur,* Carlos, who's a marvel," Peter de Gants said. "He's been singing there on Saturday nights now and then, and he's become a terrific draw.''

When they arrived at the old plantation house, beyond Santa Cruz Valley, that had been turned into a cabaret club, there were dozens of parked cars.

They found seats at a rough wooden table, on uncushioned benches. A sprawling mural depicting Carnival and other island scenes covered the wall behind them. At the far end of the room a four-piece negro band in pseudo–South American costume occupied a dais. When exhaustion seemed likely to set in, the bandleader brought the music to an end and announced the singer, Carlos.

There was a round of frantic applause as Carlos walked onto the stage and leaned up against the piano. He wore tails and a white carnation. As he faced the audience, with rather a disdainful smile on his well-cut, almost European features, Fiona drew in her breath sharply.

The singer was Carlton Marcel.

His voice was wonderful, as she had guessed it must be the first time she had heard him speak. If it was untrained, he had certainly learned to use it with terrific emotional effect. He had fire and temperament. He sang some Spanish songs and then, by loudly shouted request, a spiritual. He had the rowdy audience in the palm of his hand—you could have heard a pin drop as the last rich notes died away. Then a storm of applause broke out.

Fiona sat in stunned silence, finding it incredible that this man with the glorious voice was the one she believed had given her a dose of poison—the one Bill believed was trying to ruin Cassia.

Someone came and sat down on the bench beside her.

She started violently when a voice close to her ear spoke her name.

Her eyes widened. She turned her head sharply as if she couldn't believe her ears.

"Bill! How on earth did you find out where were were?"

Bill eyed her grimly.

"I didn't," he said. "I came here for something quite different. And now I am here, the first thing is to get you and your party of friends out, this minute."

"But, Bill . . . ."

"Don't argue." He leaned across her and spoke to Leon.

"Get out of here at once, all of you," he said peremptorily. "I happen to know the police will be raiding it in ten minutes."

"Good God, why?" cried Leon incredulously.

"That'll do for later," Bill snapped. "For now, get your party out. I'll see to Fiona."

Leon said "Righto," in rather a stunned voice, and Bill barely gave Fiona time to gather up her handbag before he seized her arm, rushed her out by a side door, ran with her to the parking lot, and lifted her bodily into the front seat of the jeep.

They were only just in time. Even as Bill started the car, there was a tearing noise of tires on the gravel around at the front of the club, the main doors were flung open, voices bellowed "Stay where you are, all of you," women shrieked, and one or two negro waiters came running past the jeep and plunged into the dark undergrowth.

Bill went speeding along, past the orange and grapefruit trees of Santa Cruz Valley, and up the long climb to the Saddle where the view looks two ways, to the valley and the sea.

There he parked the jeep and climbed out. His face, as he looked down at her, might have been carved out of teak.

"Who the devil was responsible for taking you to that sordid dive?" he demanded savagely. "Do you know what that commotion was all about?"

"No. You tell me."

"The police are raiding that place because they believe it's the headquarters of the gang who are distributing marijuana on the island. They believe Marcel is one of the ring. My police friend phoned and gave me the tip—I came to see what would happen. A good thing I did. If I hadn't, you might have had to answer a charge in court tomorrow—how would you and Dawn have liked that?"

He was furiously angry.

"But how could we know, Bill?"

"Whoever took you there should have known this wasn't the sort of place to take a bunch of young women. I'll have something to say to young de la Torre later, I promise you. Now, get in the jeep and I'll drive you back to Marjorie's. I see the lights of the police cars now, and I want to call at their headquarters and find out about Marcel before I leave for Cassia."

"You—you're going back tonight?"

"What else?"

Fiona didn't answer. Suddenly she felt utterly deflated. She sat beside him in silence while he drove, by a road avoiding the town and its revelers, along the Maraval Valley to Marjorie's bungalow. There she put a hand on his arm.

"Bill—has that man cracked the code?"

"Not yet—that's why this is so important. He's getting near, he says."

"Oh—I'm glad."

"I'll have to go. Good night."

"Good night, Bill. And—thank you."

He nodded curtly and drove off. Fiona's soaring happiness had fizzled out like a spent rocket. She stood now, clenching her hands and breathing hard, while with stormy eyes she watched the jeep till its red taillight vanished around a curve in the road.

He's hard and censorious and he's got an abominable temper, she told herself. *So why do I have to love him?*

It wasn't long before Dawn and Oliver arrived.

"Darling, wasn't that a thrill?" cried Dawn excitedly as she stepped out of the car.

"Did any of our party have any trouble?" Fiona asked.

"No. Thanks to Bill, we just had time to skip out by the side door and get around to our cars. We went off by the other road, through St. Joseph Village. Bill was an angel to come and warn us."

Fiona let that pass.

"He certainly saved us from what might have been a lot of unpleasantness," Oliver said handsomely. "Well, my lovelies, that's Carnival, that was! All over now—and so to bed, I suggest."

He kissed them both, waved an elegant hand and departed to his well-earned rest.

Dawn wasn't nearly ready to sleep yet. She sat up in bed in her frilly nightgown and prepared to indulge in lively discussion of all that had happened. Fiona was driven finally to snap off the bedside lamp.

"Do shut up and go to sleep, darling," she urged. "I'm dead and you know I've got to be up practically at the crack of dawn. Leon is calling for me at half-past seven. You, I suppose, can have a long sleep-in. What are you planning to do with your day?"

93

There was a little silence.

"Oliver is taking me out for lunch first—then he's off down south to pack and finish up generally," said Dawn at last. She added coolly, with a little laugh that seemed to tinkle in the darkness, "I'm staying on up here, Fiona darling. I've decided not to go back to Cassia."

CHAPTER EIGHT

THERE WAS REALLY NOTHING in what Dawn had just said, Fiona reflected after a moment of rather stunned silence, to cause alarm and despondency. "I'm staying on up here, Fiona darling. I've decided not to go back to Cassia." Well, that surely could mean just a prolonged visit? No reason at all for the sudden conviction that had leaped into Fiona's mind, *She's leaving Colin. She's going away with Oliver.*

"You mean Marjorie's suggested your staying on a few more days?" she asked as casually as she could manage. She wished now that she hadn't switched off the light. It would be so much easier to guess what Dawn had in mind if she could see her face. But it would look odd if she switched it on again.

She found herself waiting tensely for Dawn's reply. It came afer a pause, with another cool little laugh.

"No, darling, not Marjorie. Anyway, this house is rather too far out of town, don't you think? Actually, I'm staying with Claire de Gants."

"Oh. Any idea how long you'll be away?"

"None at all, my pet." Dawn's voice was honey sweet and very final. Fiona heard her turn over in bed and settle herself with a contented-sounding sigh.

"Go to sleep, my lamb, and don't catechize me," she went on lightly. "You said you had to be up again at the crack of dawn, and it's not far off that now. Good night. Happy dreams."

So Fiona settled herself, too, and tried to relax. But her mind stayed taut as a bowstring. She began to recall little things—how Dawn had said, when she was packing for her visit to Marjorie, "I'm going to have to take loads of clothes, even though it's only for a week"; how vividly, thrillingly alive she had seemed since they had left Cassia.

Had she, during these three days in Port of Spain with Oliver always at hand, made the decision that was going to break Colin's heart?

The question nagged at Fiona's mind between snatches of uneasy sleep.

She kept recalling, too, what Oliver had had to say on that journey up to town before Carnival, about love and marriage. "I'm a bachelor—and like it." And, "I hasten, before it's too late, to fresh woods and pastures new."

Could he have changed his whole philosophy of life—in three days? It didn't seem possible.

Impatiently as she tossed and turned and thumped her pillow, Fiona told herself that she was building up a whole edifice of suspicions and suppositions on those few casually thrown-off words of Dawn's, and on a cool, brittle-sounding laugh.

But try as she would, she couldn't unbuild it.

She listened for a minute in the darkness. Not a sound from the other bed. No doubt Dawn was sleeping as quietly and innocently—maddening creature—as a child.

There's only one thing to do, she concluded wearily. I must ask Oliver point-blank. I'll telephone him late this afternoon—he'll have arrived down south by then—and get him to run up to Cassia. He won't lie to me. And I simply must know. Because if he and Dawn *are* going away together, I've failed Colin utterly. The whole idea of my coming out here was to try and reconcile her to

Cassia. But she's so stubborn. If she's made up her mind *not* to try and work out some way of being happy there with Colin . . . .

A hot flame of indignation sprang up and burned in Fiona's breast. *I won't give up without a struggle,* she determined. *I won't let her hurt Colin so cruelly.*

That decision made, at last she slept.

If she had been less perplexed and worried, she would have loved the drive out to Cassia in Leon's open sports car in the dewy freshness of early morning.

Again it had rained a little during the night, and trees and grass sparkled with crystal drops. The countryside seemed to smile in its refreshment, and the mountains had a misty softness against the clean-washed sky. The gulf was a dazzle of sun-gilded ripples. The air, exhilarating as champagne, seemed to carry all the restless messages of spring.

Leon drove bareheaded, his thick dark hair ruffled in the wind that rushed by them. He looked virile and handsome and lovable. Fiona wondered why her heart didn't lift at the sight of him; why it only lifted— leaped—for Bill Derwent, to whom she was just a girl worth taking sailing.

Leon was singing, as he drove, for sheer joy of living. His love was beside him. He could see, in quick sideways glances, her charming profile, the tender hollow at the base of her throat, the soft flush in her cheek, her dark curling lashes. She was adorable. He was troubled by no doubts that, even if she wouldn't admit to returning his love now, she would, very soon.

Do you know what Columbus saw
When he landed on our shore?
He saw the Caribs so brave and bold,

The hummingbirds with their wings of gold . . .
He was so glad
That he called the island La Belle Trinidad.

trolled Leon, so lustily that Fiona came to with a start out of her preoccupied silence and shook her head as she smiled at him.

"Do you know what our old nanny used to say, Leon? 'Too much high spirits in the morning, tears before bedtime. Tears and tantrums, Miss Fiona, you mark my words.' "

Leon threw back his head and roared.

"Ah, but she'd never lived in Trinidad. She didn't know how wonderful you can feel on a spring morning like this one. And maybe," he added with a mischievous grin, "she was an old sourpuss who'd never known how it felt to be in love."

He turned to drop a swift unexpected kiss on her neck, just behind her ear, and Fiona said severely, "Nonsense, she was a sentimental old darling whose husband had been killed in the war. And please, Leon, keep your eyes on the road."

Not wanting to be drawn into talk of love, she asked some question about racing in the gulf, and once Leon had extracted from her a promise to crew for him in the Wednesday evening race the following week, the topic of sailing lasted them all the way to Cassia.

Both of them had a fund of knowledge and a lot of theories. Leon had made several passages with his cousins the de Gants, in their island-built sloop, between Trinidad and other islands, Tobago and Grenada and the Grenadines, and even as far north as Antigua and St. Kitts.

"Man, there's some grand sailing, and lovely little islands, up there," he told her enthusiastically. "We'll take a Caribbean cruise later on in the summer, Fiona. You'll just love it. I've always meant to have a sloop of my own built. I have all the plans ready. There are hundreds of places I'd like to show you. Man, there's a stretch of water between Grenada and Carriacou that they call Kick 'em Jenny. Two currents meet there, and the waves jump up at you madly all over the place. Gosh, it's fun sailing through that.''

Fiona, not to be outdone, told him about the Channel races—St. Albans and the swift-running Alderney, and the dreaded Portland, that isn't fun at all if you get yourself caught in it. They argued as to whether Kick 'em Jenny could possibly measure up to any of these.

"So you must promise to come with me and find out, darling,'' said Leon.

"First get your boat,'' she retorted, laughing at him, but determined not to be lured into this sort of future planning. Leon made it all sound suspiciously like a honeymoon cruise. As if everything was happily settled—which it wasn't, by any means, however hard she might wish she could find in her heart such an enthusiastic sureness as Leon's.

"May I come and share your elevenses as usual this morning?'' he asked as they turned into the jacaranda avenue.

"Please not, Leon.''

"Please, why not?''

"Well—what will everybody think?''

"Since everybody in the lab knows by now that I'm your helpless victim, darling, they'll think the obvious— that I'm pressing my suit,'' Leon told her blithely. "And so I am. I'm leaving no stone unturned. No cup of tea undrunk. And when I tell you that actually I dislike tea above all other drinks . . . .''

Fiona pulled a little face at him.

"Oh, Leon, you're irrepressible." She laughed and shrugged helplessly. How right she had been in suspecting that Leon might become something of a problem.

She wondered how he would react to the discovery—inevitable, sooner or later—that he couldn't always have what he wanted, when he wanted it. . . .

Neither Bill nor Colin had returned to the Great House yet for breakfast. Cupid greeted her with, "Good mornin', Miss Fiona ma'am, how do you do?" but his face had a worn, grayish look and all his jauntiness seemed to have deserted him.

As soon as she had finished breakfast Fiona raced out to the stables to say good morning to Sherry. The door was open, and she could hear excited yapping inside.

Then a voice said, "Come on, out you go, Julie, old girl. Take your offspring for their comfort stroll."

Her heart gave its familiar jerk.

"Bill! Hello there. Good morning," she cried impetuously.

There was a concerted rush of dog past her feet, and Bill appeared, wearing his grin and his carved dimple.

"Hello, Fiona. Growing up, aren't they? I see Leon got you back on time. As a matter of fact, I want a word with you before you go to the clinic." He was watching Julie and her litter with a sort of fatherly pride that amused and delighted her. "I'll drop you over there if you like," he offered. "We can put your bicycle in the back of the jeep. Have you had breakfast?"

"Yes. My second this morning."

"Fine. Shows you've made a good recovery from the Carnival orgy." He was looking at her quizzically over the flame of the match with which he was lighting his pipe.

"Mmm. It was a very mild orgy. Bill, what happened last night—the raid, I mean?"

100

He shrugged. "Nothing. Somebody must have warned them beforehand. The thing fizzled out rather feebly. Nobody admitted anything."

"And Marcel?"

"He faded away just as we did ourselves."

"So we still have no evidence to get him deported?"

"Not so far. Well, Colin and I have been busy doing everything possible to anticipate trouble, if it's coming. And my man thinks he's got a clue to the way the code works, he said so last night. So I'm still hoping he may crack it in time to be of use."

Fiona said frowningly, "Bill, why would revolutionaries or whoever they are, want to ruin *Cassia*? That's what I can't understand. It seems so—sort of pointless."

"Well, I don't suppose Cassia is the only producing concern they're having a go at. But it happens to be one of the most important on the island, and with the new machinery, and the new lab and clinic, one of the most up-to-date. So it's a likely target. You see, the general idea that propaganda takes is that any kind of outbreak that will embarrass the government is a good thing. Especially on an island like Trinidad—it's got big oil resources and a strategic position athwart the approaches to the Panama Canal, which makes it rather a plum."

"I see. You mean to say all this is probably just part of a general plan to unsettle the Caribbean?"

"That's it. Well, I'll put the family in now. Time to be off."

Fiona picked up Sherry, holding her up in front of her and laughing as the little creature made ineffective dabs at her with its small pink tongue.

"You darling," she said. "When can I have her, Bill?"

"End of next week, I should say." He tickled Sherry under her chin and murmured, "Little beauty."

"I just can't wait." A thought came into her mind. "Bill—will Marcel be at the clinic today?" She asked the question casually, but she didn't feel casual about it.

"That's a thing I meant to tell you. Doc McElroy understands the situation now. He sees that it's inadvisable to have Marcel around the clinic at present. So he's sending him off on a job down in Brighton. It'll keep him out of the way for a few days. You'll have charge of the keys and dish out your own requirements."

Bill turned away and whistled for Julie. She came tearing up, panting and grinning, with a lip lifted to show her small, perfect teeth. The puppies scampered after her, woofing deliriously. Bill stowed them in the stable and shut the doors. He had a curious gentleness with them, she noticed.

He closed the stable door and said briskly, "Ready to go when you are."

"In five minutes," she told him, and ran off, feeling unaccountably lighthearted, to change into her dispensary clothes.

Dr. McElroy seemed genuinely glad to have her back. She spent an absorbed morning, sending Leon away firmly when he turned up at eleven, but only by promising to go to a movie with him in San Fernando that night.

She bicycled back to Cassia for lunch and had it alone on the vine-shaded gallery. Colin and Bill had apparently lunched and gone off again.

"Too much work, Miss Fiona, ma'am," Cupid said, shaking his head. "The crop is coming in fast and there's plenty of cane this season."

"That's fine," she answered cheerfully, and noticed that his face seemed suddenly to crumple, and that he turned away quickly to hide it.

Later in the afternoon, when she got home after work, she put a call through to Oliver. The telephone stood on a carved mahogany table at the back of the hall, and she sat in the big chair beside it.

Oliver's voice asked, "Yes, Hayne here."

"Oh, Oliver, this is Fiona. I want to talk to you. It's—awfully important."

"You flatter me, my sweet."

"No, listen, Oliver," Fiona said urgently. "I simply must see you. It can't wait. Can you come up to Cassia *now*—as if you'd just dropped in for a drink? Please come, I must see you."

Oliver seemed to hesitate. Then: "But of course. I'll be with you right away."

"Oh, bless you, Oliver."

She hung up the receiver and gave a deep sigh of relief. As she rose from her chair footsteps descended the main staircase. It was Bill, in his working rig still.

"Oh—I was just telephoning," she said confusedly, annoyed to feel that her cheeks were hot.

"So I heard," he answered coolly.

She wondered what he had heard. That she was making a date with Oliver? That she *must* see him? Well, that was so. But from the way Bill was looking at her—with that hard mockery, that cynical amusement that any association between her and Oliver seemed to arouse in him—she could see that he was drawing quite mistaken conclusions.

Well, it couldn't be helped. She couldn't tell him what the trouble was—not till she had heard from Oliver's own lips that what she feared about Dawn was really so.

So she said defiantly, angered by Bill's expression, "Oliver is coming over for a drink this evening."

"Then he's all yours," Bill said in his most indifferent manner. "Colin and I are both busy. But—didn't Hayne bring Dawn back after all?"

Fiona managed to say easily, "Oh, didn't you know? She's staying on for a day or two with Claire de Gants."

"No. I didn't know. Nor, I fancy, does Colin. However . . . ."

He gave her a little shrug and went off quickly down the driveway.

Oliver must have left right away. He was with her in less than an hour.

She said gratefully, "Sweet of you. Look, let's go into the garden for a bit." That way, they wouldn't run the risk of being seen by Colin.

Oliver followed her along the path between the oleanders and ixias and hibiscus and moonflowers with a half smile on his face. He knew well enough what was coming.

"Go on, my sweet," he said amusedly. "Shoot."

"Oliver, you must tell me truly. Why didn't Dawn come back with you today? Is she—going to England with you at the end of the week?"

Oliver smoothed back his hair. "I'm afraid so," he said.

"You're *afraid* so? Then—didn't you ask her to go with you? Isn't this an elopement?" Fiona's eyes widened as she swung herself sideways to look at him.

"Since you ask, frankly no," Oliver said lightly. "Oh, of course, I adore Dawn. She and I have enjoyed a most delicious—well, call it flirtation, it wasn't anything more sinister, I assure you—ever since I first came to Trinidad. She's lovely to look at and no man could help feeling proud to be seen around with her. Her husband finds himself too busy to squire her—so what would you do?''

Fiona stared at him unbelievingly.

''That's all?''

''That's all.''

''She isn't in love with you?''

''My sweet child! Don't you realize that the strong and silent Colin is her one and only—but that she's mad as a hornet at him, hates the place he makes her live in and is determined to force his hand? She has a little money saved, it seems, with which she will buy her air passage on my plane. We shall leave together. But if you imagine I propose to seduce her en route, and feature as corespondent in a divorce case—well, my sweet, think again. I shall drop Dawn at the house of one Dr. Raymond Leigh in the New Forest and hasten on my way.''

''To fresh woods and pastures new,'' Fiona said bitingly.

Oliver laughed.

''You can laugh, but I just don't see the point.''

''The point is that Dawn believes that if Colin really loves her, he'll drop everything and come raging after us—presumably to kill me—only to find that all is well. Once she has him back in England, she aims to keep him there.''

''She's crazy,'' Fiona said flatly.

''I agree the whole scheme is crazy. I can only deplore that I've let myself be involved in it. Put it down to Carnival, and rather a lot a champagne, and the fact—let us face it—that I'm deplorably weak where any woman as devastatingly lovely as Dawn is concerned.''

''Oliver, please try to dissuade her,'' pleaded Fiona, laying a hand on his arm. He picked it up and kissed it.

"You dissuade her, and I'll be forever in your debt," he said. "Now, may we have the drink you promised, and then I must dash. I have a dinner date with an important hostess tonight."

It was no good trying to remain angry with Oliver. Fiona saw him clearly for what he was, a frivolous man, quickly bored, but with an irresistible attraction for women. He was easy to love for his gaiety and kindness, and it was hard to imagine a more agreeable or amusing friend. But under his amenable manner was a hard core of determination to remain footloose—not to be tied. It wasn't in him to give himself, without reserve, to any woman.

Even so, Fiona found she still couldn't help being fond of him. And he had at least reassured her on one point—Dawn wasn't in love with him. She was still Colin's at heart.

When Oliver had had his drink and gone, Fiona sat down in a lounge chair. It looked as if she would have to take Bill into her confidence and get him to help. There was no time to lose, if Colin was to be kept in the dark.

Thank heaven he was busy and would be till dinnertime. On the way to the clinic, Bill had told her that the installation of the new machinery had been completed, and that Colin was having his overseers and section bosses in B shed, to see it work, and to hear the engineer-in-charge explain just how it was going to speed up the processing of the cane, cut costs and provide more employment instead of less.

She ran upstairs to have her bath and to change, then returned to the gallery to wait for Bill. He looked strained and rather weary—as Colin so often looked these days.

"Finished for tonight, Bill?"

"Only till I've had some food." He went to the table

where the drinks stood, and mixed himself a rum and soda.

"Oh, but . . . Bill, I wanted you to do me a favor. I—was going to ask you to drive me to town."

He stared at her blankly. "Tonight? Impossible," he said brusquely.

"But I have to get there."

"Sorry. We're running shifts all through the night this week. For one thing it means we've at least half the factory labor under our eye, where we can watch them. And for another, the crop justifies it, anyway. But what is this, Fiona? You only came back from town this morning."

"I know, Bill but it has to be tonight. So that Colin won't know. He simply mustn't know. . . ."

Bill got up, poured out a small drink and brought it to her.

"Drink that, and pull yourself together," he advised. "Take a deep breath and tell me in words of one syllable what's on your mind."

This astringent treatment had its effect. Fiona's chin went up. She said aloofly, "If there was nobody else I could ask for help, I would. As it is . . . ."

He grinned again. "You turn to me. Well, I'm listening."

As briefly as she could, Fiona told him. "And what we have to do is stop her. Bring her back tonight," she finished succinctly.

Bill swallowed what remained of his drink and set down the glass. "Of all the fools," he said with that unpleasant edge to his voice. "And that's the woman that a man like Colin has decided to throw up everything for," he finished, with a bitterness that surprised Fiona.

"Throw up everything for? What do you mean?"

"Only this weekend, while you two were enjoying yourselves in Port of Spain, Colin broke the news to me that rather than lose Dawn, he's decided to resign his managership here as soon as this current crop has been handled. Provided, that is, that it comes up to standard. He proposes to suggest me to the company as his successor. And to take Dawn to England, to farm with his uncle of hers. *That's* how much he cares for her. That's what he's prepared to sacrifice, for a wife who isn't fit to—to—"

He stopped short. Perhaps he remembered that he was talking to Dawn's sister. He looked at Fiona now with narrowed eyes, as if to see how she was taking his strictures. To his surprise she was radiant.

She cried gladly, "Oh, Bill, but don't you see? This is going to make absolutely all the difference to Dawn. All she wants, really, is proof of his putting her before Cassia. She's jealous of Cassia, you see. She thinks it comes first with Colin. When she understands it doesn't, perhaps I can persuade her to give Cassia another chance. Bill, you must lend me a car, if you won't drive me up yourself."

Bill said curtly, "Sorry, my dear. All the cars on the place are on duty—in a park so that they can be reached immediately in case of trouble."

"You mean you won't lend me one?"

"I mean just that," Bill said calmly. "What's more, I'm not interested in stopping Dawn from carrying out her harebrained scheme for blackmailing Colin. A good thing if she does go, say I. He'll get over it and be better off without her."

Fiona controlled her rising temper with an effort.

"You must be very unobservant if you don't know yet that Colin would never get over losing Dawn," she said. "Don't you realize that she's his one and only, just as he is hers? And that you'll be doing him the worst possible service if you don't—don't help me—get me a car. . . .''

To her fury, she felt tears pricking behind her eyelids. She was going to burst into sobs, in front of this heartless inscrutable creature who was looking at her with eyes like cold steel. It was not to be borne. She jumped up.

"If you won't take me, I know who will," she gulped, and fled from the gallery and upstairs.

There was a telephone extension in Dawn's room. With shaking fingers she dialed and asked the operator for Leon's number. She was fortunate in finding him at home.

"It's Fiona," she told him.

"Darling, not to say you can't come out with me tonight?"

"No. Yes. I mean not to the movies. Listen, Leon, I have to go back to Port of Spain to talk to Dawn. It's—it's very urgent. I can't do it over the telephone—I must see her. Would you take me up there, right away?"

"But of course—anywhere—anytime," Leon assured her with his usual sweeping enthusiasm. "Will you have dinner with me in town? At Won Loo's? You like Chinese food, don't you? Fine. I'll be with you just as soon as I can make it. Bless you, darling. *Au revoir.*''

"Bless you, Leon." As she hung up the receiver Fiona was wondering again why she couldn't fall in love with Leon. He was so eager, so sweet, so gallant, too.

Bill was standing at the top of the gallery steps, gazing out into the night, when she came downstairs again. He turned at the tap of her heels on the parquet floor. His eyebrows quirked, but he said nothing.

"I—won't be in for dinner, Bill," she said. "I have a lift. I'm going off to get Dawn right away."

He saw that her chin was up in the air and noticed the defiant quiver in her voice. To her surprise he gave her a friendly grin as he said, without any edge to his voice, "Good hunting, Fiona."

His change of mood gave her courage to ask him a favor. "Bill—if Colin asks where Dawn is, will you try to stall him off? Say we've gone out, we'll be back later on. The movies, anything you can think of. . . ."

"So you're asking me to tell a white lie on your behalf, are you?" he asked with mock severity.

"Would just a small one matter—if it saved Colin's peace of mind, Bill?"

"Perhaps not. I'm not very good at fairy tales, but I'll try to think up something—to please you, Fiona."

As he spoke he thrust his arm through hers and pressed it close to his side. His fingers were around her wrist, and she was afraid her leaping pulses would betray her.

But all he said was, "Pretty, that, isn't it?" indicating the firefly ballet in the garden. He added, "Let's hope that's the only fire Cassia's going to see tonight," but skeptically, as if he had his doubts.

"Oh, Bill, do you think . . . ."

"It'll be tonight? Who knows? I'm expecting a call from our code-cracking friend any time now. Otherwise, there's nothing much more we can do except wait—and watch. Pretty trying for the temper, I don't mind admitting."

It was as near as he would get, she told herself understandingly, to apologizing for his harshness of a few minutes ago. But she didn't mind. They were friends again. They weren't fighting.

A beam from the headlights lighted up the pair of them as Leon's car swung into the driveway. He pulled up in his usual stylish manner, turned the car off and took the steps two at a time.

"Beat my own record," he told them pleasedly. "Good evening, Bill. Nice sailing breeze getting up. Ready, Fiona? Then off we go."

Fiona turned to smile and wave at Bill as Leon let in the clutch. But he had turned away and didn't see her. She sighed—it took so little to send her hopes soaring, only to be dashed to earth again. *Oh, Bill, why do I love you so,* her heart cried despairingly.

She didn't explain to Leon, on the way up, what it was all about. The fewer people who knew of Dawn's crazy scheming the better. She did, however, speak of there being no car available at Cassia, and no one to drive her, since everything and everyone there was at what Bill called "Action Stations—but not, we hope, Panic Stations!"

Leon knew about that, of course. The research staff had been warned to stand by. He himself would be taking a night watch tomorrow. It was just lucky that he was off duty tonight. He didn't seem to take the situation very seriously. He had spent so many years of his life in the midst of sugar that he regarded a cane fire as just one of those things that you knew would happen, sooner or later.

"Hello, still celebrating," he exclaimed, as they drew up in front of his cousins' home, to find three other cars also parked there. But it was only the de Gants and their friends, and Dawn, fortifying themselves with ice-cold fruit-and-rum drinks after strenuous tennis at the country club.

It was some little time before Fiona could maneuver Dawn out of the group and whisper urgently, "Can we go up to your room? I want to talk to you alone."

Dawn shrugged and said languidly. "Darling, how dramatic of you. Must we?"

"Please, Dawn."

111

"Oh, well." Dawn stood and murmured "Back soon" to her nearest neighbor, and led the way upstairs.

"Now what?" she said resignedly.

"Dawn, I know what you're planning to do. I've seen Oliver. And you can't do it. Because Bill has told me that Colin is going to leave Cassia on your account!"

"What did you say?"

Fiona repeated the gist of what she had said, with elaborations and additions.

"So you see you simply have to give up this mad scheme and come back now, tonight, before Colin begins to ask questions. You will, won't you, darling?"

To her astonishment she saw that Dawn was laughing, but happily, triumphantly—not derisively or acidly, or in that cool tinkling way that Fiona hated so much.

"So it's worked, it's worked!" she exclaimed, her eyes sparkling between the long golden lashes. "It's worked even without my going away. He loves me more than Cassia, Fiona. I come first. I've beaten sugar at its own game. Oh, wonderful, wonderful!" She caught at her short tennis skirt and pirouetted gaily around the room. "So of course I'll come back, my poppet. We'll have a lovely time together there—till the end of crop, when we'll all go sailing back home."

Fiona watched her in shocked disbelief.

"B-but, Dawn," she stammered. "You don't mean to say—when you've proved, now, that Colin loves you better than Cassia, that you're going to—to keep him to this? That you'll let him give it all up, go to England, after all the time and w-work and . . . ."

She stopped, unable to go on in the face of Dawn's burst of wholehearted laughter.

"My precious lamb," Dawn exclaimed, "Do you for one minute think that having won my two years' battle, I'm going to hand over the—the fruits of victory and say sweetly, 'Thank you, Colin, I want to do what you want, after all'?''

"That's just what I think you *ought* to do," Fiona told her hotly.

"Oh, no. Oh, no, my pet. I'll come back now, of course—but once this crop is finished with I'll keep Colin to his word. You're sure he *did* say it to Bill?" she went on suspiciously, her face suddenly looking hard.

"Quite sure."

"Oh, thank heaven. No more sugar, no more crop, no more Granny Murray with her witchlike prophecies of mischief. . . .'' She stopped short, her eyebrows coming together in a frown. "I'd forgotten about that. Mischief. Was everything quiet when you left, Fiona?"

"Perfectly. And everybody's on the alert, anyway. You needn't be scared of coming back," Fiona said with contempt. *I'm glad she's not really my sister,* she was telling herself stormily. *I shall never feel the same for her again, after this.* She was smarting with the knowledge that she had failed Colin utterly after all. This dash to save the situation had achieved nothing, except to make it all the more certain that Colin would have to give up Cassia—for Dawn. Fiona felt sick with disappointment. She looked at Dawn with angry eyes, and Dawn, stung by the look and note of scorn in her voice, hit back at her.

"Of course, *you* needn't leave Cassia, since you're so fond of it, darling," she said sweetly. "I'm sure the new manager will be pleased to let you keep your job at the clinic. He might even marry you, darling—you'd like that, wouldn't you?"

"Oh, you're hateful," cried Fiona, turning away to hide the tears that had filled her eyes, and fumbling blindly for her handkerchief.

"Here, have mine. And forget what I said, pet. I

113

didn't mean it, honestly. I was only getting my own back for that crack of yours," Dawn said contritely.

She put her arms around Fiona and gave her a quick hug, and Fiona, as quick to forgive as she had been to flare into anger, said in a choked voice, "It's all right."

She was thinking that what Dawn had said about Bill was true, anyway. She knew she would give everything she possessed to be asked to stay on at Cassia and marry him. She knew, too, that there wasn't the least likelihood of it happening. Therein lay the real sting in Dawn's gibe—that there was no future for Fiona at Cassia. . . .

It was after half-past ten before they got away. The de Gants, truly West Indian in their generous hospitality, insisted that Leon and Fiona must dine with them, instead of at Won Loo's. Then there was a good deal of argument about whether Dawn could be allowed to go at all that night. Somebody pointed out that the three of them and Dawn's voluminous luggage couldn't possibly be squeezed into Leon's sports car. Finally Peter de Gants decided to drive Dawn home and stay the night at La Rochelle. He wanted to talk to Leon about a project for an Easter cruise to Grenada, anyway.

So they started off at last in convoy, Leon and Fiona in front, with Peter and Dawn and her suitcases following.

The wind seemed to have strengthened. The road was empty except for one or two cars and trucks making their way to the capital. The villages were deserted. No roistering bands danced in the roadway now. Carnival was over for this year.

It was only when they had left the eastern road and turned to approach Cassia and the foothills, that Fiona noticed a reddish glow in the sky.

"Look, Leon, what's that?"

"Looks like fire," he said. "Up in high woods—" for that is what Trinidadians call the forest "—and the wind's blowing hard this way."

For a moment it seemed to Fiona as if her heart had stopped beating. Then it started to race.

As the road mounted they could see what was happening. The high woods were blazing at their lower edge in a crescent shape with its two horns pointing downward toward the cane fields. Already the fire fighters were at work, for the insectlike silhouettes showed black against the base of the fiery curtain.

Even as they drew nearer they saw fires spring out at other points, lower down among the canes—two, three, half a dozen of them.

"That's fire raisers at work," Leon said grimly. "Hang on, we must hurry."

He trod hard on the accelerator, and the car seemed to leap forward and fairly eat up the road.

Fire in the mountain, she thought. It's happened tonight, as Bill seemed to expect it might. They've fired the canes.

Anger, as hot as the fires she could see breaking out now in several more places, flamed in her breast against these anonymous enemies who were threatening everything that Colin—and Bill—held dear.

"Hurry, hurry, Leon," she cried urgently. Whatever was going on she wanted to be in on it, helping, fighting for the very life of Cassia.

CHAPTER NINE

As they drove along the road, Leon had to sound his horn almost continuously, for they were all the time overtaking groups of men, women, even children, all armed with sticks or sacks or spades—volunteer beaters, hurrying toward Cassia to help in fighting the fires.

Now they could hear the fire bell tolling. They could see the crescent of raging fire, thickening into a solid wedge now, at the lower edge of the high woods.

It lighted up the dark mountains with a ruddy glow, beautiful and evil. The dark figures toiling near its base looked tiny and impotent. Fiona wondered, with a sudden chill at her heart, if Bill were up there.

"What can they do, Leon?" she broke out despairingly. "How do they begin to tackle a fire like that, in such a wind? It looks—overwhelming."

Leon didn't take his eyes off the road.

"Well, you see, there's a broad earth road running right around the upper perimeter, between the canes and the first of the trees. They'll start a counterfire burning on the far side of it. It can't travel back over the road, because there's nothing for it to burn. And the beaters will control it so that it doesn't jump the road. So it'll burn slowly upwind toward the other one, which of course . . . is coming downwind. When the two meet there'll be nothing left on that line for the forest fire to burn, so it'll peter out."

Leon braked, swearing under his breath. "The trouble is . . . however many firebreaks you've burned, there's always a danger from blazing brands and drifts of sparks . . . that get tossed up into the air, fall on dry stuff like the canes and start up more fires. That's where the beaters come in again. Bill has gangs organized, chaps he can trust. They'll be rushed in jeeps or cars to each new danger point as it occurs. That's why all vehicles have been commandeered this week, you see.''

Fiona said, ''You make it sound—not quite so hopeless as it looks. But you said something about fire raisers?''

''Well, it's obvious some of those cane fires you can see are too far from the forest fire to have been caused by brands or sparks. A fire raiser waits till the main fire is well and truly going then toddles off with his little tin of kerosene and starts up another.''

Now they were too near the Great House to be able to see the fires any longer, only the red glow behind it, silhouetting the house darkly.

''We'd better go upstairs onto the gallery and have a look before we go on any farther,'' Leon suggested.

All the lights were on in the house, but there was no one around, though they could hear voices out at the rear. They went up to the long gallery beyond the bedrooms, from which they had a clear view over the cane fields to the mountains.

The raging flames consuming the base of the high woods looked even more menacing from their vantage point. Lower down in the canes, new puffs of smoke, redly lighted on their undersides, carried aloft wisps of burning cane and firefly drifts of sparks.

''How far away are those, Leon?''

''The nearest aren't more than two or three miles. Too near the bungalows and factory buildings to be comfortable, with the wind as it is. But that's being taken care of, of course.''

He gestured toward the kitchen compound. The voices they had heard belonged to a group of men standing by there, with hoses ready rigged to a water hydrant.

"There'll be parties like this at various points. They'll soak the shingles as soon as there's any danger. It's all part of the regular fire drill. Well, we'd better be moving.''

"I'll run and change.''

She found slacks and a sweater and got into them hurriedly, then tied up her hair in a scarf as protection against flying sparks.

As she turned to leave, Dawn burst into her room. She didn't seem in the least panicky, as might have been expected. In fact, she was in a flaming rage.

"The beasts, the rotten beasts!" she stormed. "How dare they do this to Colin! The whole place is going up in smoke. Oh, damn them, damn them!''

She was almost crying, but with fury, not fear. She dashed out and Fiona heard her bedroom door crash open. She hadn't been downstairs two minutes herself when Dawn came flying after her. She, too, wore slacks and a sweater and head scarf.

"Come one, let's go. Let's help to fight the fires,'' she cried. She was like a being transformed. She ran out to Peter de Gants's car. He was waiting at the wheel, and as she slammed the door shut, he let in the clutch and streaked away.

But before Fiona could leave, Cupid hurried out to them. He looked anything but stylish in old khaki slacks shirt, with a sack placed over his head like a pixie hood, but he had recovered his old jauntiness. The hangdog look of guilt and misery had gone.

"I was waiting for you, Miss Fiona," he said importantly. "I've a letter from the manager for you."

He handed it to her and she opened it quickly.

Well, it's happened, Fiona. But luckily we had warning in good time, and B shed is safe. Don't come near the fires. Go straight to the clinic. There's plenty to do there, you'll find!

Bill.

Fiona put the note in her pocket and kept her hand closed over it, as if it was something very precious.

"I'm wanted at the clinic," she said.

"Right, I'll drop you there and then see if I can locate Colin or Bill. They may want me to get extra help from La Rochelle or the Grantly place over the ridge."

As they got nearer to the clinic they began to hear the roar of the fire, muffled still by distance, but loud enough to add to the terror of the leaping flames, the billowing smoke and drifting ash and sparks.

"Just drop me, don't get out," Fiona said as Leon pulled up. "Take care of yourself . . . and good luck."

"Be seeing you," Leon answered, and roared away into the luridly lighted night.

The clinic was ablaze with lights and humming with activity. In the office she found Dr. McElroy, the clinic staff, Mrs. Murray, plainly in her element, and an assortment of patients with torn clothes, gashed and bleeding heads, cut hands and faces, contused and swollen eyes—all the indications, in fact, of having taken part in a particularly savage hand-to-hand fight.

"Come in, we'll be glad of your services, my dear," called the doctor.

"How did this happen?" she demanded of the patient

she was attending to—a young man in whose head the doctor had just put half a dozen neat stitches.

"Fellow came at me with a bicycle chain," he said with a grimace of pain as she applied a dressing.

"Poor you. Sorry, I must do this, I'm afraid. But where were you?"

"On guard in B shed. Somebody had tipped Mr. Derwent that there was going to be trouble there tonight. They were going to wait till everyone was away fire fighting, then go for the new machinery."

Fiona's eyes widened. "And . . . ?"

"So the special guard was posted. In the dark, well hidden, see? We didn't know what was coming, bombs, dynamite . . . and the funny thing was, when the toughs did turn up they carried tools, spanners and things. They had keys—didn't have to do any breaking in—and powerful torches. We kept dead quiet, watching. You'll never guess what they were up to."

"You tell me."

The young man grinned. "Can you beat it? They were starting to remove certain small but vital parts, to put the machinery out of action, see, but not destroy it. Would you ever think vandals would have had such a smart idea?"

No, but Marcel would, Fiona thought. He'd be very much alive to the excellent use the machinery could be put to, later on when his political friends took over. The last thing he'd want would be to wreck it.

"And then . . . ."

"Oh—at a given signal we jumped out and let 'em have it. Gosh, that was a scrap! That's one of 'em over there on the stretcher. The leader, I guess. We laid him out with a rugger tackle. He got a beaut of a crack on the head, too. He won't do any more sabotaging for a bit."

The man on the stretcher was Carlton Marcel.

He had lost his tinted spectacles. Now his eyes—the eyes she had never seen before—opened slowly. They recognized her as she bent over him. Such a look of malevolence came into them that she shuddered and involuntarily backed away.

Mrs. Murray came over, with her arms full of bandages, and said with a sort of grim complacence, "You see how right I was, Fiona. Mischief—I said we'd see it, didn't I?"

"You certainly did, Mrs. Murray."

"And where's our Dawn?"

"She went off with Peter de Gants to help the fire fighters. She went so fast I didn't have a chance to stop her," Fiona said with a smile. A look, half skeptical, half approving, passed over the stern old face.

"Well, well. Who'd have thought it?" Mrs. Murray said.

At length Fiona was able to take a moment to go outside and look at the fires. It was clear that they were under control now. There was still plenty of smoke, but the flames were flickering, not raging. Best of all, the wind seemed to have dropped.

She went indoors again and got a sterilizer going, and was waiting for it to boil when the door opened, and Bill Derwent walked in.

Fiona's heart started to race. She saw that he was grimy and red eyed, his hair and clothes streaked and blackened with smoke and dirt. But he was unharmed, thank God. He looked around and saw her, and came over at once.

"So you got my note? Have you got a cup of tea for a very thirsty man, Fiona?" he asked with his attractive edge of a smile.

"Of course. How is it going, Bill?"

"All over now, bar the shouting. Colin has just taken Dawn back to the Great House. We found her battling away with a sack, assisted by Peter and about a dozen field hands. Dirty as a coal miner and happy as a sandboy. Well, wonders never cease, they say."

"Good for Dawn," said Fiona, her eyes sparkling.

"And how about you?" His voice was friendly, but not in the least tender. He took it for granted she would have helped like everyone else. "Feeling you should stop?"

"Well, yes, if the doctor doesn't want me for anything else. Bill—you know Marcel is here, rather damaged?"

He nodded grimly.

"I do. Good thing. It'll keep him quiet till the police arrive. They're on their way now. They cracked the code at last. The documents prove he's employed by a revolutionary group, briefed to start riots and sabotage sugar and oil plants. He's also an active member of the dope ring. We weren't far off the mark, Watson."

"We're very clever, aren't we, my dear Holmes? But who gave you the actual warning?"

"Cupid, just after you left for Port of Spain. He'd been forced by Marcel, to hand over Colin's keys two or three times. He knew what it was all about, but Marcel promised to kill him if he talked. However, when the actual time arrived, he couldn't keep quiet. Poor chap, he was nearly in tears about it."

"Oh, I'm so glad, I didn't want him to be a—a snake

in the grass,'' exclaimed Fiona. ''He's such a dear little man.''

Bill nodded and set down his empty cup as a young police officer came into the office. At a word from Bill two orderlies lifted Marcel's stretcher and followed Bill and the officer outside.

''*Finis* to Marcel,'' Fiona murmured thankfully. Cassia—and Trinidad—certainly wouldn't be troubled by his seditious activities much longer.

''So that's that,'' said Bill when he came back to the office half an hour later. ''Now, I'm going to run Mrs. Murray home—Doc McElroy says she's had about enough. Then I'll come back for you.''

Fiona was smiling as he hurried away. No good arguing with that no-nonsense-please voice.

But in fact it was Leon who came to take her to the house. Dawn was already there: Colin stood with an arm around her shoulders, looking pleased and proud. Even Mrs. Murray looked as if for once she almost approved of her daughter-in-law.

Fiona turned to find Leon beside her. He put his arm around her, and just for a moment it was bliss to rest against him. His lips moved against her hair. He began to murmur gentle endearments, holding her closer against him. She felt drowsy and comfortable and cared for. Dear Leon. . . .

She started away from him as Bill's voice said, with that incisive—and by no means pleasant—edge to it, ''Wouldn't it be a good idea to go up to bed, Fiona? The party's pretty well over.''

''Yes. Yes, of course,'' she said confusedly.

She ran upstairs. A moment later Dawn put her head around the door.

"Hello, pet," she said smilingly. "Wasn't that a great big lovely thrill? If Cassia could guarantee as much excitement regularly, maybe I'd reconsider and stay here."

"Well, honestly, Dawn," Fiona began indignantly, then stopped short, looking at Dawn suspiciously.

"What's the joke?" she demanded.

"My dear, Colin has said his piece at long last," she replied. "It seems the loss from the fire won't be so disastrous after all, and his conscience will allow him to hand over the management to Bill at the end of June."

Fiona did her best to hide her dismay.

"So he means to leave Cassia in June? He's going to take you home, and farm in Dorset with Uncle Reggie?"

Dawn nodded gaily. "That's what he proposes. That's what he's ready to do for love of me, my pet."

"And you're going to let him do it?" Impossible, now, to keep the outraged indignation from her voice.

Dawn's charming face broke into rueful laughter.

"You can take off that governessy look, Fiona Leigh. Now that Colin has made his gesture, I simply can't bring myself to accept it, after all. Silly, isn't it?"

"Why?" gasped Fiona.

"Because tonight, when I thought that everything was going up in smoke—all that Colin's forebears and Colin himself had made with their lives—I found I couldn't bear it. I suddenly seemed to see Cassia with Colin's eyes. I understood what it meant to him, and how he would be without it. That's why I got so mad, and had to rush off and fight for all I was worth."

This is a new Dawn, one I didn't know before, Fiona thought, amazed.

"The funny thing was," Dawn went on, "that when I

124

was out there, I wasn't scared at all. I actually enjoyed it. Crazy, isn't it? And crazier still that when at last Colin offered me the chance to go, I found I wanted to stay—believe it or not."

Her charming face was alight with laughter—at herself.

"Care to be a godmother, pet?" she went on cheerfully. "Because if so, you might go and buy some knitting patterns for little garments, and some two-ply wool in pastel shades. You know I never could knit, so it'll be up to you."

Fiona burst out laughing.

"You're incorrigible," she said. "And I'm so delighted I don't know how to tell you. But I *must* go to bed, I really must!"

WITHIN A VERY FEW DAYS life got back to normal—so much so that the following Sunday the club held its usual sailing event. Bill and Fiona raced, and won again, and after a picnic lunch set sail for the five toy islands that ride the gulf like little ships.

It was another perfect day, with just the right amount of wind and very little sea. A blue, sparkling day of clear horizons and hot, but not too hot, sunshine.

Fiona had the tiller, till they reached the islands and the bay where they could drop anchor.

It was a charming little spot, with a sloping beach where they could bring the *Alouette* up close enough for them to wade ashore.

"Come up on this rock, you can just see the Bocas at the entrance to the gulf," Bill said.

She started to climb up to him, but set her foot on a loose stone, stumbled and gave a little cry. He reached down and pulled her up beside him. He didn't let go.

Suddenly he bent down and kissed her. His lips were hard and urgent, and she felt her own responding eagerly. Then coolly he let her go.

What's happened? What went wrong? she was thinking miserably. We were kissing, it was wonderful and then . . . .

Presently Bill asked, his voice cool and detached, "You're going to marry Leon, aren't you, Fiona? It's the talk of Port of Spain."

She colored. "The talk of Port of Spain? Well, it's not true."

"But Leon says—"

"I can't marry him."

He turned and put a hand under her chin, turning her face up so that the sunlight fell on it.

"Why can't you marry him?"

"I don't love him."

"Do you love—anyone else?"

"Yes, I do."

"And will you marry him, then?"

"No, Bill. He—doesn't love me."

It seemed a long time before Bill moved. Then he turned abruptly and drew her to him. His lips sought hers and a rush of emotion overwhelmed them.

"Do you think I'll let you go?" he demanded roughly when at length he lifted his head. "I love you, Fiona. You'll stay here and marry me." His lips were gentle as he kissed her again, until hers gave their eager response; then they pressed down hungrily, urgently.

"Fiona, can you forget this other chap?"

"Never."

"You could try."

"No, Bill, you idiot. Don't you know? It's you I've been in love with, almost from that first day when we quarreled about Dawn—remember?"

126

"I remember. Perhaps I fell in love with you then, too."

"You never showed it. You were—horrid to me!"

He threw back his head and laughed aloud.

"That, my little one, was plain jealousy. I didn't know it then, but I'll admit it now. Of Oliver, of Colin because I knew you loved him once, especially of Leon, who seemed so suitable for you in every way."

"Poor Leon. I shall have a terrible time with him!"

"Don't be too sorry for him. He's a de la Torre, and all of them love easily and often; it's part of their charm, I always think. So you'll kindly stop thinking of him, think only of me, you sweet, funny little thing."

"Yes, Bill, only of you," she said docilely. Under her breath she added, "My darling," as he drew her close again.

What readers say about Harlequin romance fiction...

"Harlequin books are the doorway to pleasure."

"They are quality books—down-to-earth reading! Don't ever quit!"

"A pleasant escape from the pressures of this world."

"Keep them coming! They are still the best books."

*Names available on request.